THE EMERALD KEY

BY

MARK FREDERICKSON

AND

MELORA PINEDA

BLUE TULIP
PUBLISHING

The Emerald Key
By Mark Frederickson and Melora Pineda
Published by Blue Tulip Publishing
www.bluetulippublishing.com

THE EMERALD KEY
Copyright © 2015 MARK FREDERICKSON
AND MELORA PINEDA
ISBN-13: 978-1522782766
ISBN-10: 1522782761
Cover Art by Jena Brignola

For Sara and Delaney, may the adventures never end.

CHAPTER ONE

THE AXE FELL ON its unsuspecting victim. Across the field, he saw her body fall. His bloodied hands outstretched to the sky, "Why, God? Why?" He struggled to raise his battered body from the blood-soaked ground. With every breath, he dragged his soon-to-be corpse across enemy lines. Smoke from the battle created a thick screen of effective cover as he slithered into their makeshift headquarters tent, unnoticed. He could see the generals gathered at a table reviewing strategy. Evading their detection, he slowly inched his way closer to them, blood trickling down his forehead into his eye, making it difficult to see. He only needed a few more feet to strike the crippling blow to his enemies. With his last ounce of energy, he pulled the pin from his micro-grenade and swallowed the device. The enemy spotted him and immediately advanced with their weapons drawn.

"For you, Emma," he said with his final breath. They aimed their weapons at him, but it was too late.

Seconds later, the entire headquarters camp exploded. He was gone, but so were his enemies.

The screen went black.

The lights flicked on and bleary-eyed eighth graders sat up in their seats, some needing to wipe the drool off their desks. Steve Kealing, a nerdy kid from the AV club, turned off the projector.

"Okay, class, pack up your things before the bell rings." Miss Brooks waddled across the room and wrote *Have a wonderful summer vacation* on the whiteboard. "Now before you go, there's one thing I'd like to say to you."

The bell rang, and thirty-six tweens jumped up and ran for the door.

Laci Reece remained in her seat after the classroom had cleared out, her nose buried in a book. She unconsciously wiped her long brown locks of hair away from her face as they fell forward and grazed the pages as she read.

Penny Wright popped her head inside the door. She was unarguably the most fashionable girl in school. Her bright blue eyes blinked as she shook her head, causing her golden blond hair to sway back and forth. She wasn't surprised to find her best friend still in the classroom. "Lace, what the heck are you still doing in here? I was a block away before I realized you weren't behind me."

Miss Brooks turned around after erasing her message off the whiteboard. "Laci? The bell rang."

"Oh, I didn't hear it," Laci said as she filled her oversized backpack with her pile of books on mythical creatures and other fantasy-related subjects. "I hope you have a nice summer, Miss Brooks," she said as she walked out and closed the door behind her.

"You didn't hear the bell ring?" Penny asked Laci as they walked down the formidably empty hallway.

Laci shrugged.

Penny knew it was because her friend was more interested in reading books than doing just about anything else. "I guess this is why you have a platinum-card rating at the local library."

Laci smiled in her shy way, her brown locks falling into her face again.

"You've got to start paying attention to reality, girl. You're getting a little too old for those fantasy books. No knight in shining armor is going to jump out of your book and ask you to the dance," Penny said.

"Easy for you to say. Everyone wants to ask you to every dance," Laci said. "Even that boy you made eat sand in kindergarten."

"I had to feed him the sand. He was being mean to you," Penny said.

That had been the beginning of their unlikely friendship, and Penny knew she and Laci would stay friends forever. She respected her friend and their differences.

There were many differences. Penny was a natural athlete; it was obvious in the way she moved, but not in the way she dressed. She was the standard by which fashion was judged in Midville. Finding clothes in this sleepy town proved to be one of the bigger challenges in her life.

"Lace, what are you planning to wear on Sunday?" Penny asked. She adored her friend, but Laci dressed for comfort, not for fashion.

Laci shrugged again.

"We'll need to discuss that tonight and find something appropriate. From my closet," Penny said.

Laci was a bit shorter and thinner than Penny, lacking the athletic build, but Penny knew she could find something that would make her friend look pretty.

The girls leisurely walked down the road. Unexpectedly, wetness sprayed all over their shoes, and they jumped back to avoid the water balloons that pelted the asphalt in front of them. They heard laughter from behind a tree ten yards ahead and across the street. Ethan Hendricks stepped out from behind the towering oak. His tall, lanky build and spiky, product-filled hair didn't give the menacing effect he'd hoped for.

Penny scoffed at the attempt. "Is that all you got?" Her head roll completed her mocking tone.

Ethan smiled at Penny's brashness.

She knew it was one of the reasons he'd had a crush on her since the third grade.

He reloaded another water balloon into his homemade, hospital-grade rubber-tubing slingshot and let it fly. He fired directly at Penny, but she was too quick and ducked. The balloon flew over her head, drenching the Welch's mailbox, soaking the contents inside.

Buzz Chang stepped out from behind another tree. His small stature was even less menacing, and his slingshot appeared to be even more homemade than Ethan's. In fact, Penny was almost afraid for Buzz's safety when she saw the rickety contraption. Rubber bands held together a funnel Buzz had stolen from his mother's kitchen.

"You girls are toast. No matter how fast you run, I'm going to nail you both. C'mon, I dare you to run. I never miss a shot."

Penny stood her ground and replied, "We're not going anywhere, Buzz. Why don't you stop talking and try and hit us? Oh, and try not to kill yourself in the process."

Laci laughed while she shrewdly slid herself behind the protection of Penny.

Ethan also laughed, visibly irritating Buzz, who quickly fired two water balloons at once toward the girls, but his plan and his slingshot both failed miserably. The balloons fell short, bouncing on the soft grass unbroken.

Laci ran to pick one up, but her heavy bookbag slid over the top of her head and sent her crashing to the ground.

Both the boys doubled over in laughter.

Laci picked up one of the balloons and hurled it in the boys' direction, only to come up woefully short. The boys cracked-up to the point they were rolling on the grass. Their laughter quickly halted as Penny grabbed the remaining balloon. Before they could scramble to escape her wrath, she fired the water balloon with so much force and accuracy that Ethan didn't even have time to close his mouth. It exploded in his face, drenching him. Buzz laughed so hard he fell back down on the ground, dropped the rest of his balloons, and soaked himself.

Laci yelled, "Let's get out of here!" and began to run as fast as she could while carrying a thirty-pound backpack.

Laughing the whole way, the girls soon found themselves in the safety of Grandma's yard. Penny swung open the rickety gate and headed to the front door but stopped for a moment and looked at the house.

The architecture in this little town was from a time gone by. Narrow streets hosted picket fences and solitary mailboxes at the ends of long driveways. The warm breeze moved through the thick, green trees and created a canopy of dancing shadows over the sidewalk. The neighbors were friendly, but the distance between them assured privacy.

The sleepy town had only had one bit of excitement over the past twenty years, and every time Penny walked through that rickety gate, she thought about it. Robert Stratford, who had been an upstanding member of the community, a church leader, and said to have been one of the most interesting people in this small town, had just up and left his wife, Elsie, and their daughter one day. No note. No warning. No trace. The gossip surrounding that event lived on for several years, and at times had taken on a life of its own, but just like the paint on the mailboxes and the picket fences, it too had faded away.

Robert was Penny's grandfather, or would have been if he had stuck around. She'd often envisioned what life would have been like with him. Things were changing, however, and she was going to spend the entire weekend at her grandmother's house to help her get all the final preparations ready for Grandma's wedding to Roy Rastaban. Although Penny wasn't a fan of the reserved fiancé, he treated her grandma well, so she didn't voice her apprehension. Keeping her mouth shut when she was unhappy was no small feat for

Penny. This time, however, she'd refrain from speaking her mind because she was actually selfishly looking forward to someone else spending his or her Saturdays helping Grandma clean and shop.

Laci, being the good friend that she was, agreed to spend the weekend with Penny, helping her with all the arrangements.

"What do you think your grandmother is going to want us to do?" Laci broke the silence following their escape from Ethan and Buzz.

"I don't know. But what I do know is that I, that is, *we*, have to do all of it. Smelly Roy has no family at all coming to the wedding. We're going to be running around all weekend. Woo-hoo, what a way to start summer vacation." Penny gave her best sarcastic smile.

Laci smiled back.

Penny knew she understood her frustration and her sarcasm. Some people accused Penny of having an attitude, but she was aware Laci knew the truth. Penny would do anything for her friends and family. She'd stood up to more than one bully for Laci in their long and steadfast relationship.

"I don't know what smell you're talking about, but I can't wait to find out," Laci said, and they laughed; a natural ease to the friendship the two opposites endured.

Growing up in the same small town as her grandmother was a double-edged sword. Early on, it had meant a built-in babysitter for Penny's parents. Hanging out together had allowed Penny to get close to her grandmother, as well as having given Elsie some companionship. Now that Penny was moving into her teenage years, the prospect of spending a Friday night with Grandma just didn't hold the same appeal for her as it had when she was five. Although not a big admirer of Roy's, she was relieved that more of her time would be her own.

That thought was smacked out of her head as another explosion of water hit the doorjamb just as she reached for the bronze knob. Without even looking up, Penny yelled, "Ethan!" and swung open the door.

CHAPTER TWO

LACI RACED INTO THE house, but Penny took her time, well aware the enemy wouldn't dare fire now that the door was open. The excitement of the water-balloon assault quickly subsided as Penny sauntered through the door of her grandmother's house. A wave of apprehension washed over her as she stepped on the worn wooden floor. It creaked under her feet as she walked into the foyer. *Am I irritated that she's marrying Roy because he smells and is less exciting than a rock? Or am I actually upset that I won't be seeing my grandma as much anymore?* Penny quickly shook off that notion as she saw Fluffy, Grandma's Persian cat.

"Hi, Fluffy. You're going to miss me coming around all the time, won't you?" she said as she stroked the cat's thick, white fur, releasing clumps of the shedding winter coat into the air.

Laci tried to pet Fluffy too, but Fluffy jumped up onto the bookcase. "That cat doesn't like me," she muttered.

"It's not you. She's shy around most people except me and Grandma."

"Grandma and me," Laci corrected.

"Give it a rest, Lace. It's summer vacation."

While walking across the bookcase, Fluffy was startled when she knocked over a framed embroidery, and she quickly

8

scampered off. Penny flipped over the frame and set it back up. A layer of dust existed beneath it, not the dust-free rectangular patch under the other framed pictures on the bookcase. "This is new, I think," Penny said to Laci. "Of all the times I've been here, I've never seen this before."

As Penny curiously studied the timeworn handiwork, Grandma walked in from the kitchen. Her stereotypical apron and chained glasses hanging around her neck were a comforting sight to Penny.

"Oh, there you are, Penny. I thought I heard you come in. Come on and give your grandma a hug."

Penny shuffled over and hugged her grandma. Although she acted tough, the years they'd spent together had created an inseparable bond.

"Hi, Laci, I'm so glad you could come and spend the weekend with us and help us out with all the festivities."

"It's my pleasure, Mrs. Stratford," Laci said.

Mrs. Stratford. The words hung in the air.

"I guess this will be one of the last times I hear that name." Grandma seemed to go into her own world as she finished her sentence.

Sensing her grandma might start to get emotional, Penny quickly changed the subject. "Grandma, what's this?" she asked as she pointed to the embroidery. "I've never seen it before."

"Oh, yes." She reached for the frame and brought her glasses up to her nose for a clearer view. "This is Roy's family crest."

Penny took a closer look. "It looks like—"

Grandma put the frame back on the mantle and cut off Penny's train of thought. "I just thought it would be nice to have Roy move some of his things in before the wedding. He doesn't like to accumulate stuff, unlike your grandfather who collected everything. So, he's just bringing over a few things to make it feel more like *our* home instead of just *my* home. It's nice for me since I've lived here for so long and have filled almost every space already. You know, I got this ceramic cat when we went to visit the Amana colonies. Do you remember that?"

Seizing the moment to cut off her grandmother, who she knew could go on and on if allowed, Penny spoke up. "Oh yeah, I remember, Grandma. Good times, good times."

Laci smirked, which Penny recognized was in appreciation of her sarcasm.

"So what would you like us to start doing?"

Grandma looked as if she was reading a to-do list in her head. "Oh yes, yes, thank you. Why don't you girls put your things in the bedroom upstairs, then go into the attic and get a stack of lace tablecloths for me and bring them down. I want to use them at the reception. They should be somewhere near the window."

"Okay, Grandma," said Penny as she and Laci headed up the stairs.

"Don't forget to iron them. They will need it."

Penny was already at the top of the stairs, with Laci trying to keep up.

"Your grandma said we should iron th—" Just then Laci tripped on the top step and face-planted into the upstairs hallway. Her backpack smacked her in the head as it hurled forward. She gathered herself up, trudged into a bedroom, and tossed her backpack onto the bed. The weight of it made the mattress bounce and the bed creak. Several books spilled out, including one on dragons.

"What did Grandma say?" asked Penny.

"She said we should iron—"

Before Laci could finish her sentence, Penny noticed the books sprawled out on the floral bedspread. "Oh no, there will be none of that this weekend! Put those things away."

Laci's head dropped. Penny could see her disappointment and then realized Laci had spotted something of interest.

"Fine, I'll put the books away for the weekend, but you have to put on that dress first," Laci said to Penny, who gave a look of complete disgust in response.

She'd been dreading that issue since she'd found out she would be in the ceremony. Hanging by the door to the attic were three dresses for the wedding. The first was Grandma's beautiful ivory-lace dress. She'd had it for decades, and the simple beauty matched her style to perfection. The second was a simple blue chiffon dress for Penny's mom and, last but not least, was the most hideous, bow-infested, poufy, little girlish, princess-pink, taffeta dress for Penny. Some cousin of some sort, whom Penny wished had never existed so that she wouldn't be stuck with this appalling dress, had worn it to Grandma's wedding to Grandpa.

"You're just mean" was all Penny could manage to say as she turned her back to Laci.

Laci was snickering under her breath as Penny pulled off her clothes and slipped the dress over her head. "Ta-da!" As she spun around, there was something delightfully childish about the way she looked, and at age fourteen, there was nothing good about looking delightfully childish.

"I love it!" said Laci. "I think you should wear it again on the first day of high school, or maybe your soccer banquet — no, soccer tryouts!"

"Are you done?" An exasperated Penny stood humiliated, wondering what she'd done to deserve the torture that would soon befall her once her teammates saw her wearing it. It was a small town, and some of them would be at the wedding.

Laci snatched up Penny's pants. She rifled through the pockets and found her iPhone. She quickly snapped a picture of Penny, took a good look at it, and an evil smile spread across her face. "Hello, Facebook."

"Laci, you have a mean streak in you," Penny said, and they both started laughing. "C'mon, let's find those tablecloths." The girls ran up the stairs to the attic.

The space was almost dark, the only illumination coming from a hanging, solitary, dim light bulb and one window at the opposite end of the room. The peaked ceiling had dark wooden beams. The air was stale, and the smell of dust, mothballs, and possibly cat pee permeated their senses. As their eyes adjusted to the dim lighting, they scanned the filthy boxes in the room, searching for the tablecloths.

"It's a little creepy in here," Laci said as she pawed her way through a few cobwebs. She started thumbing through a stack of various old clothes, spotted something white, and reached for it. She startled Fluffy, who'd followed them up but now bolted for the other end of the attic, causing Laci to yelp and lose her balance.

"We are looking for tablecloths, not the cat," Penny teased.

Laci gave Penny a sneer and straightened herself up. A glimmer of metal shot out from under the floor. Moving closer to investigate, Laci's face was soon pressed against the dirty floorboards.

"What are you looking at?" asked Penny.

"There's something under the floorboards, but I don't know how to get it out."

Penny looked around, grabbed a large gargoyle bookend, and was about to bring it crashing down onto the floor.

"No!" yelled Laci. "Don't. You'll ruin it. There has to be a way to get to it."

Penny nodded, acknowledging the logic of Laci's point.

"Here, help me clear some of this stuff out of the way," said Laci.

Penny picked up some boxes and dumped them off to the side.

"Hey, one of the boards is cut," Laci said. As she ran her hand along the wood, she felt something cold and realized a ring was embedded in the wood. It had been painted over to look exactly like the floorboard. She pulled on the ring and the floorboard came up. "Look, it's a secret hiding place. How cool."

"What's in there?" asked Penny.

"It's a metal box," Laci stated and pulled it out of its hiding place.

"Not much of a buried treasure," said Penny, "What's in it?"

Laci handed it to Penny, who tried to open it, but it seemed locked. With no key or key latch to open it, she grabbed the gargoyle again and raised it above her head.

"Stop. You know smashing things isn't always the answer," said Laci.

"It usually works for me. And you didn't have a problem when I smashed that apple turnover in Jeremy Duggan's face when he was making fun of you."

"Well, that time, smashing was the perfect thing to do. What a jerk Jeremy is. Here, hand me the box."

Penny handed it to her, and Laci studied it closely. The rusty metal box was simple except for an elaborate gold locking mechanism. "I've seen one of these before. Well, I've read about it." Laci took the box and flipped it around so the back hinges were facing her. She pressed the two hinges simultaneously toward each other, and the lid to the box popped open. "It's a false hinge. You think it opens on the other side, but it's a trick to keep people from getting into it."

The girls took the box over to an old rolltop desk that looked cleaner than the other dust-covered objects in the attic.

They opened the top, and the inside of the desk appeared to have recently been ransacked. "I wonder what your grandma was looking for," Laci said.

"Probably the tablecloths, like we should be. So what's in the box?" Penny asked.

Laci pulled out an old brown leather book. The edges were curled with wear, and the pages were yellowed with age. She opened it carefully, turning each page. "It's a journal of some sort." Immediately, she began to read it, muttering "Monumental" from time to time.

Bored with watching her friend read again, Penny thumbed through the objects in the box. She was left speechless when she found a large, green jewel about the size of a walnut. As she held it up to the light, the stone's brilliance had an almost blinding glow to it.

Laci was too busy devouring the journal to notice, so Penny dropped it onto the book. Mesmerized by the brilliance of the stone, Laci said, "Monumental."

"It's like a lost treasure. OMG! This means we're rich. This thing has got to be worth a buttload of money." Excitedly, Penny paced back and forth.

"It can't be real," said Laci.

"It looks real," Penny replied.

"Nobody puts a real jewel like this in a box in the attic." Laci handed the jewel back to Penny to return to her reading. Penny peered into the box, searching for other treasures, but before she found anything else of value, Laci called out, "Bring that jewel back here. Look at this."

"What is it?" asked Penny.

"This jewel... I think there's something about it in the journal." On one page there existed an outline curiously similar to the emerald. She placed the stone on the page. Underneath the outline was an inscription. Laci squinted, mumbling the words as she read them.

"What?" Penny couldn't understand what she was saying.

"Girls?" Grandma yelled from the bottom of the stairs.

"Coming!" Penny yelled down as she scanned the room for the tablecloths. She spotted them, grabbed the pile, and tossed half onto Laci's lap.

"Have you girls found the tablecloths yet?"

"Yes, Grandma, we're coming down now."

Laci quickly returned the journal and the jewel into the metal box and put it back into its hiding place.

"Come on, we need to get these to Grandma before she makes us clean the litter box or something," Penny said.

As the door slammed shut and the girls raced down the stairs, a flash of light filled the attic, followed by the yowl of a cat.

CHAPTER THREE

THE GIRLS BOUNDED DOWN the stairs; Penny's poufy pink dress flopped up and down with every step. They turned into the living room, proud as could be now that they had actually found the tablecloths, and presented them to Grandma, who was sitting in her well-worn, pastel green, La-Z-Boy rocker, mending a small tear in a pair of Roy's pants.

Sliding her glasses down her nose, she glanced up and said, "Let me see. Oh, yes, those are the right ones." She looked back down at her sewing and then her head lifted again, "Oh Penny, you're wearing the dress. You look so lovely in it."

Penny watched memories fill her grandmother with happiness as she once again told the story how her niece had worn that dress when she'd married Grandpa, before he'd disappeared. The room was filled with an uncomfortable silence when the story ended.

Laci stood frozen, looking confused as to whether she should continue with the tablecloths now that the grandpa-subject had been initiated.

Grandma looked completely lost in thought, and Penny didn't dare ask for more details on her grandfather's disappearance since it made her grandmother too sad to talk about it.

What she knew she'd picked up through the years from overhearing her mom, grandmother, and neighbors as they'd discussed the disappearance. She had tried looking up old newspaper articles at the local library, but they had been superficial when it came to the facts of the case. At the time, it was the biggest scandal to hit those parts, but with so little to go on, the speculation had subsided, and the story had disappeared when the Welch's prize-winning heifer had been struck dead by the snowplow.

Penny had heard mentioned that he'd been a loving husband and father, and everyone who knew him considered him a good man. There had been no indication that anything had been wrong with their relationship, his work, or his finances.

With Grandma now silent, Penny turned to Laci. "We should iron these."

They walked to the other room. Penny took out the ironing board and iron and set them up in the dining room. She was an expert, as ironing had become one of her go-to chores on the weekends when she visited Grandma. The iron was so old there were rust stains around the holes where the steam came out.

"Isn't that going to stain the tablecloths?" Laci asked, but Penny assured her it had never left a mark on anything.

"I know. I think this thing is older than Grandma," Penny said.

"Maybe, for a wedding gift, I should get your grandma a new iron! Say... something from the last thirty years." Both girls laughed.

"Nice, Lace, a little sarcasm from you. I like it."

Though old, the iron heated up quickly. Penny felt the heat radiating toward her, so she carefully moved it to the edge of the ironing board, making sure not to come in contact with the hot metal surface. She spread the first lace cloth on the board. Years of practice had honed her technique, and she used slow and steady movements as she pressed the lace fabric back and forth, gently flattening out the creases.

As Laci picked up the first finished cloth and hung it over the back of a dining room chair, she said, "Oh no Penny, I think you burned it!" She handed the tablecloth back to Penny, who examined it but saw no burn marks.

Penny smelled the tablecloth. "It's not this, but I smell it, too." They glanced around the room but saw nothing amiss. Penny sniffed the iron, but it wasn't that either. She headed to the hall where the smell was stronger and realized where it was coming from. "Laci, it's coming from upstairs. C'mon."

The two girls raced up the stairs to discover smoke seeping out from under the door to the attic.

"Don't open it," warned Laci.

"I'm not. Call 911." They raced back down the stairs, and Laci grabbed the kitchen phone. She was talking to the emergency operator before she was out the front door. Penny quickly helped her grandmother out of the house.

Living in a small town meant they had to give up some conveniences that a big town could offer, such as the big bargain stores, national chain restaurants, and, as Penny had discovered, it was hard to find cutting-edge clothing; however, there were some advantages such as the fire department was not only close by, but almost never busy.

Moments after the call, the fire truck, six firemen, and practically all the equipment the town owned arrived on the scene. The rush of their big, yellow, fire-retardant uniforms created a breeze as they raced by the girls standing on the front lawn. Penny found it strangely exciting, yet terrifying at the same time. The girls watched as the last fireman disappeared through the front door. The hose wound through the grass like a giant serpent. A yell came out from the attic, and the flat gray snake suddenly plumped up as if it had just eaten a huge meal.

In no time, another yell bellowed and the snake deflated. It was over in just a matter of moments, but that was all it had taken for half the neighborhood to gather outside.

The girls and Grandma impatiently waited. Grandma was still holding the needle and thread to Roy's pants, which were tucked under her arm. The concerned neighbors kept asking if she was all right, but Grandma appeared too fixated on the house and didn't seem to hear much of it.

Finally, the fire captain emerged from the house and headed straight to her. "Hi Elise. Don't worry about it. The house is fine. It was a small fire that seemed to be localized on one of the beams in the attic. What's strange is I can't seem to find the cause of the fire."

Elise stared at the fire captain, looking dumbfounded as he continued to explain. "It's as if the rafters just caught fire. We detected a slight methane gas smell, but there are no gas pipes up there, and had it been a gas leak we'd be looking at a lot more damage."

Grandma looked at the girls. "Did you girls see or smell anything while you were up there?"

"No," said Penny. "It was just a bunch of clothes, a desk, things like that, and we definitely didn't smell anything other than the usual musty attic smell."

Penny noticed Laci's backpack hanging on her shoulder. "When did you have time to grab your books?"

"When a house catches fire, you grab your prized possessions. I wasn't about to let these catch fire. Some of them belong to the library."

"Sometimes it amazes me we're such good friends," said Penny.

The firemen were exiting the house when Penny looked over and saw a tear rolling down her grandma's face. "Grandma, what's wrong? He said the house is fine."

Grandma took a few seconds and turned to her granddaughter, "It's just that now there's another unsolved mystery, and I'm at the center of it."

Penny put a comforting arm around her as they waited for the firemen to finish up.

As soon as they were given permission to go back inside, Roy pulled up in the driveway. His brownish, greenish car had an odd frog-in-the-mud look to it. The car door opened with a loud creak, and Roy stepped out but was besieged upon by Brutus, the next-door neighbor's Chihuahua, who raced up and started biting Roy's pant leg. This was the usual welcome Roy got from Brutus. It was a Hatfield-and-McCoy-type relationship with the hatred for each other flowing both ways. Brutus had a death grip on his pants as Roy unsuccessfully tried to shake him off. He grumbled as he kicked. "You stupid little dog."

Penny and Laci couldn't stop laughing at Roy who shook his leg vigorously, but Brutus still managed to hold on.

"Stop it, girls," said Grandma as she reached down and emancipated Roy's pants from Brutus' jaw. "Now, now, you have to be nice to Roy. He's going to be living here," said Grandma as she caressed Brutus' tan, smooth head.

Roy stepped away from Brutus and directly into a small, steamy pile Brutus had just left on the lawn. "I'm going to kill that dog."

"You'll do nothing of the sort," scolded Grandma. "Poor little Brutus is just lonely. The Rileys are so busy with their business that he gets left outside all day with no one to play with and gets bored. He just needs a little attention. Don't you, Brutus? You just need some love." Brutus snuggled up to Elsie, and the two headed for the house as Roy frantically tried to clean his shoe off on the grass outside.

Grandma was thanking the firemen as she walked into the house when she suddenly asked, "Where's Fluffy?" She quickly grabbed one of the firemen. "Did you see my cat, Fluffy, in there?"

"No, ma'am, no cat. He probably—"

"She, Fluffy is a she," Elise corrected him.

"She probably ran outside once she smelled the smoke. Animals have a much better sense of smell and know to get as far away as possible. I'm sure she'll come back soon as she's hungry."

"Okay, thanks again," said Grandma. She, Penny, and Laci all entered the house with Roy close behind them.

"I'm going to see what happened," Roy said as he stepped into the foyer.

"Oh, no you're not!" Grandma said as she pushed him back outside. "You're cleaning that shoe out back before you do a thing. The house is already going to smell like smoke. I don't need you spreading poop all over the place as well."

The girls giggled as they did every time Grandma used that word.

Roy grumbled as he and his poop-covered shoe turned around and headed to the back yard.

Grandma chased after him and handed him a roll of paper towels while saying "Don't come in until it's completely clean."

CHAPTER FOUR

THE DOORBELL RANG. Penny ran from the kitchen. "I'll get it." She opened the door to see Ethan and Buzz staring at her with dopey grins. *Is that how they usually look?* She wondered. "What do you want?" she asked.

Ethan and Buzz just stood there. They looked disappointed and confused by the not-so-warm-welcome from Penny.

"Well?"

"We want to know what happened. Why was the firetruck here? Did you do something stupid? Or was it your grandmother? Old people start fires all the time. They forget that they left something on and they—"

"Left something on!" Before Buzz could finish his ramblings, Penny gasped and ran to find the iron was still on and burning hot. She quickly unplugged it.

The boys used the opportunity to let themselves in. "Well, what happened?" Ethan asked.

"Was it the iron? Did you start a fire with that iron?" Buzz endlessly questioned.

"Did I say you guys could come in?" Penny asked.

"Well, you didn't say we couldn't, and you did leave the door open, so we just kind of thought you meant come in," said Buzz.

"Fine then, come in."

Ethan sheepishly asked again, "So what happened?"

Penny eyed him for a moment. "You can come up, but there's not much to see." Laci appeared from the kitchen, and the two girls led them up the stairs.

"Wow, Penny, that's a pretty poufy dress you have there," said Ethan.

Penny spun around and tried to give Ethan an intimidating stare, but it was hard to be tough in a giant pink marshmallow dress. In all the excitement, she had forgotten she still had it on.

"You got something to say about the dress too, Buzz?" Penny glared at him.

For possibly the first time in his life, he didn't utter a word but just shook his head no.

Penny turned back around and led them up the stairs. As they entered the attic, a foul smell was now obvious. "What's that horrible smell? Does your grandmother keep dead bodies in here, or rotten eggs? Wow, that smells bad. Does it always smell this bad up here?" Buzz asked.

"No, Buzz, it doesn't always smell like this up here. In fact, we were just up here, and it didn't smell like this before the fire," snapped Penny. She walked over to the solitary window to open it and let some fresh air in. It was old and had been painted so many times that the thick paint prevented it from sliding up easily.

Ethan went over to help her, but she blocked him and managed, with some difficulty, to get the window up. "I can do it myself. Thank you."

"I didn't mean anything by it. Girls just don't usually do things like that."

"What? Like open windows? Thanks, but I'm not a helpless maiden," Penny said.

"I didn't mean that," Ethan responded.

"Get a room, lovebirds," Laci said.

Penny shot a glare in Laci's direction, but Laci quickly turned and walked away.

Buzz gazed up at the burnt rafters, examining the damage. "You could have used a few water balloons up here, huh? Well, so long as Laci wasn't the one throwing them." Buzz obviously thought his comment was exceptionally funny and started laughing.

Laci picked up an old purse and threw it at him but missed.

Both Buzz and Ethan laughed.

"Not cool," Penny said to Ethan.

He stopped laughing and punched Buzz in the arm. "Hey, shut it."

In response to their glares in his direction, Buzz began to wander around looking at random things, rubbing his punched arm.

"What started the fire?" Ethan asked.

"The fire department has no idea. We had just been up here getting some tablecloths, and there was nothing strange or anything," Penny answered.

"The journal!" exclaimed Laci as she ran over to make sure the journal was intact. She pulled up the floorboard and removed the metal box while brushing water off the top. She opened it to find the journal was undamaged.

The boys gathered around her to see what had gotten her so excited, but before they could see anything, Laci was off again like a shot, racing down the attic stairs.

"Where's she going?" asked Ethan.

Penny shrugged as Laci came racing back up the stairs carrying her backpack.

"Of course. You almost went ten minutes without your books," said Penny sarcastically. She watched as Laci pulled out a book and thumbed through it, repeatedly tucking her brown locks behind her ears as they fell onto the pages.

Laci opened the journal to the page she'd been reading right before they'd left the attic.

"Laci, what is it?" asked Penny.

"I'm not sure yet. Maybe nothing."

"Hey, guys?" Buzz was making noise again, but at that point, it was obvious the others had tuned him out. "Guys," Buzz said again.

Laci pulled out the jewel and Ethan's eyes grew as wide as saucers.

"It's not real, dummy," Penny stated with authority.

"I knew that," he claimed.

"The journal says that for the world to remain in balance, one must exit when another enters. I know it's in here somewhere. There were some other words that went with it," Laci told them.

"So what does that mean?" asked a confused Ethan.

"I'm not sure, but..." Laci trailed off, as she returned to reading the journal.

"What, you think something in that journal started the fire?" asked Ethan.

"Guys." Buzz was still trying to get their attention, but to no avail.

"How can a book start a fire, unless you set the book on fire?" Ethan asked.

"I'm not saying the book started the fire, but we read from the book, we left, then a fire started. There may be some connection," Laci said as she searched through more pages.

"Yeah, Laci, it's a magical fire-starting book. Did you get that at the local library?" Ethan joked.

"Do you even know where the library is?" Penny quipped back at him.

"Right here." Laci found the page, but before she could say anything else, Buzz interrupted louder than ever.

Coming from a family of eight children, Buzz was often lost in the mix, so he'd become a master at making noise. "Guys, I think I know what started the fire."

In unison, and in a slightly irritated tone, they said, "What is it, Buzz?"

Buzz pointed up to the rafters. Jaws agape, they saw a dragon, about the size of an overfed bulldog, clinging upside-down to one beam.

They were all rendered speechless until Laci questioned, "Is that what I think it is? And if it is, how could the fire department miss that?"

Almost on cue, the baby dragon scampered its short legs over to line up its body with a large beam, creating an instant camouflage.

Laci smiled and said, "That's how. Monumental!"

Although she was smiling in awe, the other three were screaming in terror. Their screams caused the dragon to run in small circles on the ceiling. It let out a tiny squawk in fear.

"What's going on up there?" Grandma yelled from downstairs.

"Nothing, Grandma, just saw a spider, that's all," Penny quickly covered.

Grandma asked Roy, who had finished drying off his shoes, "Can you go upstairs and see what all the fuss is about?"

"Sure. I hope the spider's not too scary," Roy said as he headed up the stairs.

The sound of his footsteps put the kids in a panic. "What are we going to do?" asked Penny.

Laci just stared back at Penny. "Quick, think of something!"

CHAPTER FIVE

THE FOOTSTEPS CONTINUED UP the stairs. Penny looked up at the ceiling and could see the dragon. She tried to convince herself that if she didn't know it was there, she would not be able to see it. The doorknob to the attic began to turn, and the group held their collective breath. Laci spotted the journal and stuffed it and the emerald into her backpack.

The door flew open, and Roy stomped in. "What's going on up here?"

The gang of four looked at anything but Roy as they fumbled for an excuse to explain the noise. Ethan said, "I thought I saw a—"

As he finished his sentence with "—snake," Penny piped in with "spider."

"Well, what is it, a snake or a spider?" asked Roy.

"Did you know that one time a ghost in Oregon lived in an attic just like this one?" clamored Buzz.

Roy looked confused as to what the kid was talking about and why he wouldn't stop. "This ghost was waaaayyyy awesome. You see, it wanted to be a mom still, 'cuz it had been a mom, but it wasn't a mom anymore cuz it was dead, but it still wanted to be a mom, so it would go around and try and take care of the kids in the house, like put them to bed and cook them meals, but I don't know how it would cook them meals 'cuz it was like a ghost, and how could it turn on the stove without hands? That makes no sense, but anyway, this ghost was like trying to be a part of this family, and it lived in an attic that looked just like this."

Roy stared dumbfounded as Buzz kept rambling. "I swear it was true, no lie. I saw it on an episode of *Super Paranormal Facts,* which is like my favorite show. Okay, not my favorite, but pretty close. Well, maybe it is my favorite, so it has to be true. And one time they had this giant salamander that ate a man—"

"Stop!" yelled Roy, who'd clearly reached the end of his patience. The kids watched as Roy slowly investigated the room, sniffing the air as he walked along. "What's that smell?" he asked.

Buzz immediately blurted out, "Ethan farted."

"That's what we were yelling about, really," Penny lied. "Well, that and the spider." She looked toward Ethan to confirm he would take that humiliating blow for the team. She was pleased to see him hang his head in shame.

Roy ignored them and continued his search around the attic, smelling the air as he walked along. As he walked over to the window, the metal box that had contained the journal caught his eye. He picked it up and slowly examined the contents.

Laci looked like her heart was going to jump out of her chest.

Penny worried to herself. *What if he knows about the journal? What if he sees the dragon? What am I saying? We just discovered the journal, and who would think that a mythical creature was hiding in your attic?*

Roy stepped toward Laci. She inhaled and squeaked as the air sucked in. The room went silent as he poked at the items in the box.

"What's this?" He questioned them all but looked at Laci.

Laci didn't speak.

Buzz and Ethan looked at Penny, who calmly replied, "It's mine."

Roy looked suspicious of her answer.

"It's stuff I collected when I was a kid. Well, a little kid. I thought I lost it." She pulled it out of Roy's hand. "Thanks for finding it for me." Penny quickly walked away with the box and told him, "We promise to stop yelling."

"Yeah, we promise," Ethan added.

This seemed to pacify Roy enough to get him to take one final look around the attic. As he headed for the door, he said, "Your grandmother has had a trying day. I'd appreciate it if you kids could behave yourselves."

Penny said, "We're sorry. We'll keep it down."

Roy turned around and exited the attic, leaving the door open behind him.

"Wow, Penny, you came up with that lie awful quick," said Buzz.

"It wasn't a lie. Laci and I found it. It was in my grandma's attic, and I know it wasn't hers, so that makes it mine."

"I wasn't criticizing you. I was just impressed. Do you think we should have told him about the dragon? Maybe he would know what to do," Buzz said.

Ethan laughed a little and asked Buzz, "How many dragons do you think he's taken care of?" He turned to Laci and said, "Laci, you probably know more about dragons than anybody around here. If anyone can figure this out, it's you."

Penny could see Laci's shy smile through her long brown locks of hair that messily covered her face. That made Penny smile too.

Laci opened her backpack and pulled out one of her books on dragons.

Ethan looked over at Penny and asked, "Does she always carry books about dragons with her?"

Penny nodded.

Laci was clearly oblivious to the conversation as she was completely engrossed in her book. "You guys, listen to this. Dragons sleep on piles of jewels because jewels aren't flammable, and they can breathe fire in their sleep."

Penny glanced up at the burnt rafters. "Well, that makes sense."

Laci continued, "A dragon's hollow bones are stronger than steel."

"I knew that," said Ethan.

"Sure you did," Penny scoffed.

"What? I heard it somewhere."

"Continue, Laci," said Penny. She stepped behind Ethan to distance herself a little more from the dragon clinging to the charred beams.

"Smoke rising out of a cave indicates dragons inhabit it. Young maidens are their favorite food." Laci flipped through her dragon book. "Drinking dragon's blood provides courage and the ability of flight, but only temporarily."

Ethan looked at Penny. "You drink first."

Laci continued to read aloud. "Many dragons are shape-shifters. While in human form they can produce human offspring." They all stopped and looked up at the dragon.

"Nope, still a dragon," said Buzz.

Laci read, "The female dragon is larger and more aggressive than the male. Born harmless, all dragons eventually develop a craving for flesh."

This caused the other three to take a step away from the dragon.

Laci said to them, "Guys, this one is still just a baby. I don't think you have anything to worry about."

"Not yet," said Buzz.

"Here it is!" She read, "They smell horrible because of the methane they contain to make fire."

The air was filled with a sense of *no kidding* as Laci continued to read.

"Dragon's only die in battle. Never reveal your full name to dragons. It allows them to see into your soul and adversely affect you."

Buzz took this opportunity to introduce the dragon. "Hello, little guy, or girl, this is Ethan Hendricks."

Looking shocked and possibly in fear that the dragon was crawling into his soul and reading his deepest darkest secrets, Ethan blurted out, "He's Buzz Chang."

Buzz laughed. "That's not my real name, dummy."

Ethan looked to Penny for help.

She shrugged.

Then he turned to Laci. She looked stumped, too. Although they had lived in the same neighborhood all their lives and gone to the same school, they didn't know his real name. His parents called him Buzz. His teachers even called him Buzz.

"Sorry, Ethan can't help you," Penny said.

Laci went back to reading the dragon facts and finally reached one that could help in their current situation. "In order to defeat a dragon, one must use trickery or chicanery. Their size and strength hinder physical destruction. I think maybe we'll have to trick the baby dragon to get it contained."

"We're gonna kill it?" said a shocked Buzz.

"No!" Penny snapped at him then turned to Laci and asked, "That's not what you meant, is it?"

"Of course not. I meant to confine it so we can study it," said Laci. She opened a small notebook and started to take notes and observations regarding the dragon.

Penny saw what she was doing, grabbed her by the shoulders, and shook her in a moderately violent manner, speaking loudly and slowly as if Laci was a deaf, foreign-exchange student. "You're aware that we can't keep it! This is not a stray cat! Perhaps you've noticed what it's done to the house in the five minutes it's been here? Did you forget that they breathe fire in their sleep and think young maidens are tasty?"

Snapped back into reality, Laci picked up the journal. She started to flip through the pages but began to look uneasy. She glanced up to see all eyes on her. "What are you looking at?" she asked.

"You're the dragon expert here," said Buzz. "Remember, you said they like fresh maidens! That's right, ladies, this sucker is gonna grow up and have you for lunch. Well, Laci will probably just be a small snack."

A barrage of *shut ups* were hurled in the general direction of Buzz.

Penny turned to Laci. "What do we do?"

Daunted by the pressure, Laci started to sink down into the floorboards as she flipped through the pages of the journal. She'd never been the one to make the decisions. She'd never been in charge of anything important. Penny had always taken care of those things for them. Although she was flattered by the confidence Penny had in her right now, Laci wished it wasn't such a life-and-death situation. She was stock-still as the other kids looked to her for answers.

Penny asked, "Laci, why are you reading the journal and not the book about dragons? We need to figure out what to do with it."

Laci sheepishly looked at Penny. "Well, since I can't keep it, and I can't study it, I need a way to get it back home. But the problem is I don't know where it came from."

"Well, won't the dragon book help you with that?" Ethan asked.

"Hey, guys," Buzz interjected, but no one responded.

"That can't tell me where this dragon came from. The last book I was reading before we left the attic was this journal. Next thing I know, a dragon is burning down the house."

"Hey, guys," Buzz interrupted.

"Not now, Buzz," said Ethan. "Go on, Laci."

"So, I thought there might be some answers in this journal." Laci buried her face deeper into the book.

"Hey, guys!" yelled Buzz in a panicked voice.

"What, Buzz?" Penny impatiently responded.

Buzz pointed to the ceiling — the empty ceiling.

"He uses camouflage. He's up there somewhere," Ethan said with doubt in his voice. The four of them frantically looked around but found nothing.

"Uh-oh!" said Ethan.

"What do you mean uh-oh?" asked Penny.

Ethan pointed over to the open window with one hand and used his other to point to the open door.

"We're in so much trouble," said Penny.

The dragon was gone.

CHAPTER SIX

SCAMPERING LIKE FRIGHTENED RABBITS; the kids came barreling down the stairs to the first floor. Penny, leading the way, came to a grinding halt as she ran into a furious-looking Roy, who was standing at the bottom of the stairs, arms crossed, brows furrowed. "I thought I told you kids to keep it down," he scolded them.

The rest of the gang slammed into Penny, who did a remarkable job keeping her composure.

"I'm sorry, Roy. Ah, Mr. Rastaban. I promise we'll be quiet. We just need to find something."

Roy eyed Penny suspiciously and asked, "Find what?" She had accidentally piqued Roy's interest again. As it turned out, they weren't as good at being inconspicuous as they thought. Since no one replied, Roy asked again, "What are you looking for? Maybe I can help you find it."

"Nothing," said Laci as she scanned the ceiling.

Roy glanced up to see what she was looking at.

"Nothing that you can help us with," said Penny, realizing Roy was getting more suspicious by the second.

"I suggest you kids go outside to look for whatever you're not looking for," Roy said.

Quickly coming up with a reason to stay in the house and search other areas, Laci said, "I need to pee." She ran into the bathroom and immediately pulled open the flowery shower curtain. Empty. She quickly opened and closed every cabinet, but no luck; then she started to check every drawer, which turned out to be pointless. "Think, Laci, think," she said to herself. Laci had spent a lot of time alone growing up, so it was not uncommon for her to talk to herself, even aloud. Finding nothing, she popped back into the hallway. She was met with the eyes of the entire group, including Roy. She walked quickly past him and said, "Wrong bathroom." She ran up the stairs and out of sight.

Roy looked at Penny, who said, "She likes the other bathroom better. She's weird that way."

That was all the invitation that Buzz needed to start a story. "You know, I had a friend once who couldn't go to the bathroom unless he was at his own house. True story. He would have to hold it and hold it all day then run home after school." Buzz had Roy cornered with his story, giving Penny and Ethan a chance to look around.

Ethan looked in the living room but didn't see anything knocked over or any place for the little guy to hide. Penny shot past a distracted Roy to investigate her grandmother's bedroom. She flipped up the white-lace sham and began her search.

Buzz was going strong with his distraction of Roy. "Then they had the problem of summer vacations. It was fine if they didn't go anywhere, but what happens if they go to Hawaii or something? You can't hold it for a week. Believe me, I've tried."

Roy shot Buzz a horrified look.

"That's another story, but you know what they did? They got a motorhome and convinced him that the motorhome was his new home so he could go to the bathroom in it. That way they could go on vacations and things. Oh, and this other guy—"

Laci came down the stairs and signaled to Ethan by shaking her head.

"No what?" asked Roy who was trying to inch away from Buzz.

"No... problem. That one did the trick," said Laci.

Penny entered from down the hall. The blank stares on their faces revealed they still couldn't find the dragon.

Buzz was still talking, but Roy was no longer listening. "And those zits wouldn't go away. I mean, he tried everything."

"Outside, now!" demanded Roy.

On their way out Buzz said, "I need a jacket." He opened the closet and looked around, saw nothing that shouldn't be there, and closed the door.

Penny leaned in close to Buzz and whispered, "Nice cover, Buzz. How exactly did the dragon open the closet door?"

Buzz looked frustrated as his ideas rarely earned him any respect. "Well then, where did it go?"

"The door. That's it, Buzz. You're a genius," said Penny, remembering the cat door that led from the kitchen out to the back yard.

"You called me a genius," Buzz said, beaming with happiness.

Penny smacked his arm to get him to follow her. She could tell he was completely clueless as to why he was a genius.

She ran into the kitchen with Buzz behind her. Both Laci and Ethan followed her lead.

Her grandmother was stirring a pot of stew on the stove. "Penny, what are you kids doing?" she asked.

As she flew by, Penny yelled, "I'm sorry. We'll be done in a minute."

"Wait! Penny, the dress!" Grandma yelled as they all ran past her, but it was too late.

Penny was out the back door and into the yard looking around wildly, wondering what kind of trouble the dragon could possibly be causing in the neighborhood.

Yapping like crazy, Brutus immediately accosted them, startling, and stopping them in their tracks.

Penny ran past him, but the other three found themselves temporarily frozen.

"Roy's right. This thing's a pain," said Buzz. He kicked his foot to get the dog away.

Ethan started to laugh at Buzz fighting off the dog but stopped when he noticed smoke coming from the detached garage.

"Penny, look!" said Ethan as he pointed.

She looked over at the garage and, with Laci and Ethan, sprinted off to see what was causing the smoke. Although she was pretty sure she already knew.

Buzz tried to run, but Brutus continuously tangled himself in Buzz's every step, tripping him repeatedly. "Seriously?" he yelled at the little dog.

They entered the garage, and since there hadn't been a man around for years, it hadn't seen a lot of use. Penny's grandmother had been too sad to go in there and stir up old memories. There were trashcans, an old workbench, and tools hanging on hooks above it, typical of any garage in this town; however, everything had a thick layer of dust covering it. The tool bench and tools obviously hadn't been used in over a decade. There were plenty of cobwebs and old leaves that had blown in through the years. One of the piles of leaves was smoldering. Penny pushed Ethan out of the way so she could stomp it out. They frantically looked around, but saw no sign of the dragon.

"It obviously started the fire. Where is it?" Laci asked.

Simultaneously they remembered to look up.

CHAPTER SEVEN

THE BABY DRAGON WAS clinging to the rafters of the garage like one of those scared cats in a cartoon. Its big black eyes looked down at them as Laci wondered how the heck they'd get that thing down.

The dragon cocked its head to the side and let out a small high-pitched squeak, like a twenty-pound future-deadly parakeet. The dragon's lip curled up at the end as if it were trying to smile at them.

In unison, the group said, "Aw," but with every second they stared into its eyes, the deeper they were entranced by it.

Laci shook her head, remembering an important fact she had neglected to tell the group. "Stop looking at it," she shouted. "It can hypnotize you if you stare too long into its eyes." She shoved each of her friends to break their eye contact with the baby.

"Wow," said Buzz. "I was so relaxed."

"Exactly," said Laci. "That's how they get some of their meals. They surprise them, and the prey is so stunned that they stare at the dragon, not knowing what to do. They eventually become so relaxed that the dragon eats them with little or no resistance."

The thought of being eaten alive snapped the group back to reality.

"What, we can't look at it? How are we going to catch it if we can't look at it?" Ethan shrieked.

"Don't freak out," said Laci. "You can look at it, but try to avoid staring into its eyes for too long. It may not be trying to hypnotize you. It's just a baby, but it still has the power to, so we need to be careful."

Ethan looked slightly embarrassed. Not only had a baby hypnotized him, but he'd overreacted to it. "Well, c'mon, we need to capture this thing," he said, recovering his dignity best he could. He, Penny, and Laci looked for anything in the garage that might help them with their mission.

Buzz had been told to watch the dragon so they wouldn't lose track of it again. He snapped his head back and forth to avoid staring directly into the dragon's eyes. It started to grunt and pulled its head back. "Um, guys, I think the little fella is planning to— what the heck? Oh no! I think he's gonna sneeze!"

Although it was an adorable squeaky noise, a dragon sneeze did, in fact, produce flames. Hot air swept over Buzz, covering him completely in soot. "Ah, man."

Ethan let out a small snort in response to Buzz's calamity and continued scanning the garage for something that might be useful in his quest to capture the dragon. He spotted an old, dented, metal trashcan. He dumped the contents onto the floor and walked back over to where Laci was searching.

The entire time they'd been in the garage, Penny had stayed conspicuously quiet. Ethan poked her in the arm and said, "C'mon, let's try and get him."

Penny kept looking into the distance as if she was still in a trance.

Ethan started to shake her. "Penny, wake up!"

"I'm awake, you butthead!" chided Penny.

"I'm sorry, it looked like you were still in a trance," Ethan apologized.

Penny stared at Ethan and asked, "Then what?"

Three blank faces stared back at her.

She continued. "Okay, we catch him, then what? We take him to the pet store, the zoo, the fire department? He's a dragon! He didn't just wander in off the street, now did he?"

A deafening silence filled the garage. Laci looked at her friend, waiting for instructions. Penny had always been the leader, either by default or by her own sheer will. Being an only child, Penny was used to getting her own way, and most of the people in her life let her lead the way. Her pragmatism had served her well in this leadership role.

"Penny is right," said Ethan.

Normally, he would agree with Penny no matter what she said, but Laci noticed his sincerity.

Penny had their attention but wasn't speaking.

Not one to usually break the silence, Laci spoke first. "Well, what are we going to do? We can't just let it live in the garage and risk it getting free to run around town."

"You're right, Laci. It doesn't belong here, so where did it come from?" Ethan asked.

Buzz chimed in, "I've been wondering that the whole time."

The other three glared at him.

"What? I have," he said as he turned back to keep vigil on the baby.

Penny started to pace back and forth under the dragon and said, "Somehow that dragon got here, and I can't believe I'm going to say this, but it has to be some sort of magic."

Laci grabbed her backpack, pulled out her *Dragon Field Guide,* and started flipping through the pages.

"That's a real book?" Buzz said with amazement as he wiped the scorched mess off his face and clothes.

"It's coming in rather handy today, isn't it?" Laci replied. "I've read in here where it talks about what magical creature's dragons are, and that's why so many of them were hunted. People tried to harvest them for their magic. Not unlike they do now with rhinos for their horns or elephants for their tusks."

"So," Penny interjected, "you're saying that it could have somehow magically been sent here?"

The boys nodded in agreement, mostly because it didn't pay to argue with these two, and they didn't have any better explanation to offer.

"Not sent here," said Laci slowly. "What if it was summoned here?"

The thought just seemed to confuse them all.

"What do you mean? We summoned the dragon here?" asked Penny.

"How could you do that?" questioned Buzz.

Penny and Laci stared at each other. Laci knew they were thinking the same thing. "The journal." Laci threw her dragon book back into her bag. Her excitement was obvious to the others because she would rather eat a mound full of Brussels sprouts — and she despised Brussels sprouts — than to ever throw a book. She pulled the journal out.

"What did you read, Laci?" asked Penny.

Laci was frantically flipping through the pages until she came to the page she had read before they left the attic.

"What does it say?" Ethan asked.

"I'm not sure," replied Laci. "It's all in code, and some are just notes in the margin." She flipped the journal back several pages and froze.

"What is it?" asked Penny.

"This is the first page of the chapter I was reading before we went downstairs. I didn't realize the book had chapters. Look!" Laci turned the book around for the rest to see.

At the top of the page it said *Botkyrka*, then underneath the title was a crude drawing of land with mountains, rivers, and valleys, but flying high above the mountains were several unmistakable shapes: dragons. In the far right bottom corner was another drawing of a huge dragon with two heads but with human legs.

Buzz was the first to notice it. "What the heck is that?" he asked.

Laci took a closer look. "I don't know. It's not in any of my books."

Buzz looked up at the dragon still clutching the rafters of the garage. "Well, if that thing sprouts human legs and jumps down, I'm out of here."

Ethan started to freak out. "So are you telling me you guys brought a dragon here through a book?"

Penny and Laci looked at each other, said nothing but obviously understood each other.

Penny said, "I think so."

"Okay, so if we brought him here, then it makes sense that we can send him back," Laci said.

"But how?" Ethan asked.

Laci continued to read the journal. "Ah-ha!" she said as she jumped up and grabbed her backpack. Rummaging through it, she found the metal box and pulled out the large emerald. "Now, this is just a guess, but I think that the journal by itself and the jewel by itself are harmless, but if you put them together, the magic happens."

"Like dragons appearing in your attic?" asked Ethan.

"Yes, something like that," said Laci. "I think these things created a portal between our two worlds."

Penny asked, "So do you think we could open the same portal and send the dragon back?"

Laci, feeling confident, said, "I think so."

"I need more than 'I think so,'" said Penny.

"I'm trying Penny. It's not like I open portals every day."

Buzz muttered under his breath, "No, just today."

Penny shot a look to silence Buzz.

All eyes focused on Laci, who was feeling the pressure and starting to sweat, but she was beginning to understand that she was the one who, although unintentionally, had opened the portal to begin with. She regained her composure and leaned into the journal, with a strand of her hair flopping on the page.

Penny did what she did best: took control. "Okay, while Laci is figuring out how to send our little friend back home, we need to capture it so we can make sure it goes back to where it came from."

Buzz started talking again. "I wonder how it travelled. Do you think it was like a portal taxi or maybe a limo?"

Penny gave him that look again and Buzz immediately shut up.

"Alright, Ethan, you hold the can, and Buzz and I will direct the dragon to you. When it gets to you, put it into the trash can and close the lid," Penny said.

Ethan looked like he hated the plan but responded with a winning attitude. "Sounds like a great plan, Penny."

Penny was holding the trashcan lid with both hands and noticed the dragon appeared mesmerized by his reflection. "Good dragon... Aren't you cute? Yes, just follow yourself... Come on, little guy... down here near the trash can..." Penny coaxed it slowly down the beam.

Laci was still reading the journal and trying to retrace her steps, flipping through the pages while the boys and Penny worked on the capture. She continued to read one passage several times. "Listen up!" She read, "As one thing enters, another exits."

Penny stopped. "Did something leave when the dragon came in?" she asked as she looked around the garage. Her eyes met with Laci and Penny cried, "Fluffy!"

"Don't worry. I'm sure Fluffy is fine," Laci said, trying to convince herself of it, too.

Buzz was using a broom to coax the dragon toward the trashcan; however, by swinging the broom he was stirring up dust in the garage. The dragon sneezed and burned up the broom.

Ethan laughed at his friend, grabbed a metal rake, and tossed it to Buzz. "Try this instead."

The dragon sneezed again, only this time it was straight at Ethan. He reacted quickly by covering his face and turning away; however, he was unaware that the tips of his spiky haircut had become singed. "See, Buzz, that's how you do it. You don't just stand there with your jaw wide open and get burned up. You turn away and stay perfectly intact."

"You're almost intact," Penny said as she looked at his hair.

"What? What happened?" Ethan looked panicked. He patted down each and every part of his somewhat-polished look to check for damage. When he got to his hair, which used to stand just a little higher and a little blonder, he gasped.

"It's okay, Ethan. I kind of like it better this way," Penny said.

The dragon shifted and moved down the beam.

Ethan stopped focusing on his hair and grabbed the trashcan again. The dragon was still interested in his reflection, so Penny started to pull the lid farther away from him. She could see that his grip on the beam was loosening. "Come here, boy... Yes, look at yourself in the mirror... You're so cute..."

The dragon slipped off the beam, and Ethan caught him in the can. Penny immediately slammed the lid down tight.

"We got it!" Ethan shouted.

Penny turned to Laci and said, "Okay, girl, you're up."

Laci felt ill. "I think I understand what I need to do," she said as she shrunk into her blue hoodie.

"You've got this. You'd better make it quick, though, because my guess is that trashcan isn't going to hold for long, and he's going to be mad," Penny said.

Laci set up the journal with the jewel in place and stared at the page.

"What are you waiting for?" Ethan asked as he sat on the can and struggled to keep the lid down as the can rattled underneath him.

Her focus and concentration weren't broken by his comments. Laci mumbled incoherently, and a glowing ball with wavering lines through it appeared in the back end of the garage.

"Grab the can!" yelled Penny.

The boys tried to lift the can and pour the dragon into the orb, but Buzz was struggling with the shifting weight of the dragon. The dragon appeared frightened and was screeching to the point of distraction, as it tried to dig deeper into the trashcan.

Penny pushed Buzz out of the way and took over his side of the can.

Laci was still trying to maintain her concentration on the words she was reading while holding the journal and balancing the jewel on it.

"I think it's working. I can feel the suction," Ethan said as he started to pull away from the orb, looking slightly frightened by the sheer power it held.

The force started to suck all three of them in with the dragon and the trashcan. Their feet slid across the floor of the garage. It was impossible to stop; they knew they were getting sucked in. Laci reached down and grabbed her backpack just in time.

Buzz, who had moved to the other side of the garage when Penny pushed him away, watched what was happening and said, "I'm not gonna be left here alone to explain this mess!" He ran toward it and dove into the orb with his friends. The trashcan lid fell with a crash and rolled across the floor until it stopped right in front of Brutus, who sniffed it, whimpered, and ran off.

Seconds later, a singed and startled Fluffy appeared from the closing orb, followed by four confused-looking kittens. They began to lick themselves to clean their smoking fur. Fluffy headed over to the sunlight coming in from the door and curled up into a ball to rest. Her four new friends joined her.

CHAPTER EIGHT

TRAVELING THROUGH A PORTAL wasn't as fun as it had sounded. First of all, it was pitch-black; the *can't see your hand in front of your face* kind of black, and it was cold and windy. That combination of darkness, wind, and chill made it extremely disorienting to Laci. Then began the really fun part: the pressure. Not the kind of pressure felt when taking a test; this was physical pressure. It felt like her whole body, except for her head and feet, were stuck inside a tube. Glancing at her friends, she thought they looked like four giant Pixy Stix with heads and feet floating through a dark, cold tornado. *This is portal travel*, she thought. *This stinks*.

Following that ordeal was the landing. The best way to describe it would be to compare it to a scoop of ice cream hitting the floor. Laci ungracefully landed with a giant thud that knocked out what little breath was left in her after the Pixy Stix squeeze. Finally, it ended with a blinding light, going from complete darkness into bright sunlight. As her eyes adjusted to their surroundings, she was treated to an amazing sight. They had landed in a lush green countryside covered by a beautiful blue sky with big fluffy white clouds. They sat on top of a grassy knoll high enough to give them a view over the tall trees to the landscape below. Sluggishly they started to stand.

"Ow, I hit my head when I landed." Ethan broke the silence. He looked to Penny, who was still speechless, shaking her head, trying to clear the cobwebs

She looked out over the forest around them, spotting a small rustic looking village in the distance.

"Laci?" Penny turned to find Laci was no longer at her side, as she had been when they were dragged out of her grandmother's garage, but was instead following the baby dragon. Her backpack was already torn open, with books spewed all over the ground. She had her notebook and pencil in hand, frantically scribbling down observations after every movement the little dragon made.

"What do you eat? Hopefully not young maidens yet." Laci smiled as she picked up specimens of plants and feathers she'd found. She stuffed them into her pocket with amazed curiosity. "Monumental." She seemed oblivious to their situation and possibly dire circumstances.

Buzz, who appeared to be regretting his decision to leave the garage, finally found his never-ending voice. "That sucked! I felt like I was going to lose my lunch." He looked around at the landscape but didn't recognize any of it. "This was a bad idea. I didn't have to jump in, but I did. Very bad idea. I could've stayed home. I could be safe now. I want to be home. I'd rather be fighting with my brothers. I'd rather have my mom yelling at me. I'd give my Xbox to my little brother if I could just shut my eyes and click my heels and get home." Buzz squeezed his eyes shut as tight as he could and began to bang his heels together as hard as possible.

Ethan looked at him and asked, "What the heck are you doing?"

Buzz glanced around. It hadn't worked. "I was trying to get back home," he said.

Ethan gave him his *I can't believe we are friends* look.

Buzz hung his head, and walked off.

Penny grabbed Laci and said, "What are you doing? Get your head back in reality, girl."

That got Laci's attention because any emotion outside of happiness or sarcasm was foreign coming from Penny. Laci looked back and forth between the dragon and the others. It was sinking in that the situation was her fault; she was the one who had read from the book. She was the one who'd gotten them into this mess.

Penny asked in a softer tone, "Laci, where are we?"

Laci looked at the landscape in front of her. Nothing looked familiar. "Well, I'm not sure," she said as she thumbed through the journal. "If I were to take a guess, I would say that we're back in the land where the baby dragon came from."

Ethan seemed a bit annoyed, "No kidding. What land is that, Laci?"

Laci started to feel the pressure; not the Pixy Stix kind of pressure, but the unprepared-for-a-test kind of pressure and that was something she almost never felt.

"I don't know," she said. "I thought that once he got here, he would run off to his home, but he hasn't left, so maybe this isn't the right place."

They all looked over at the dragon rolling around in the grass.

"Maybe he doesn't live here. Maybe we're on the wrong planet!" Ethan yelled.

"Don't be ridiculous. We're not on another planet," Laci said.

"Yes, well, then where the heck are we? Last I knew they didn't have dragons living anywhere on EARTH!" Ethan shouted.

Penny turned on Ethan. "Don't yell at her. We may not know where we are, but she was able to open that portal again and get him out of my grandmother's garage. She's smart. She'll figure this out. Soon, I hope."

"Um, guys!" Buzz was crying for their attention. The baby dragon had now attached itself to Buzz's leg and was jumping up and down.

"OMG, Buzz, you're a mom." Penny started to laugh at Buzz who was trying to run with a small dragon attached to his leg.

"Get him off me!" he begged. The weight of the dragon forced Buzz to trip, but the dragon held on strong.

"Buzz, I think Penny's right. I think it does think you're its mother," Laci explained. "It's called imprinting. The first thing an animal sees is usually its mother, so they have an immediate attachment to her. Maybe it saw you first when we were in the attic."

"Well *he's* attached to me, and I want to get him off, and stop calling him an it," said Buzz. "I can tell he's a boy by the way he blinks. It's very masculine."

"We obviously need to get it back to its mother," Laci said. "I mean, *his* mother."

"What happens if we can't find his mother?" Buzz panicked.

Laci shrugged but knew that it couldn't be good.

Penny interjected, "No, Laci, we need to get back home. I'm sorry if the dragon doesn't find its mom, but it seems quite capable of protecting itself." She glanced over as Buzz was trying to kick the dragon off his leg, much like Roy and Brutus but without the hatred. Instead, fear percolated on Buzz's end, and love and adoration on the end of the dragon. There was some drool on Buzz's jeans where the baby was now licking him. "We need to focus on getting the heck out of here."

Laci realized that her dream of palling around with a dragon was going to have to be put on hold, and she needed to concentrate on getting everyone back home safely. She opened the journal again, flipped to the page with the outline of the jewel, and said, "I guess we try it again, but this time without the dragon."

CHAPTER NINE

SOME PEOPLE DO THEIR best work when the stakes are at their highest. Laci wasn't one of those. She excelled at school, rarely bringing anything home below a ninety-five. That was due to the fact that Laci was absurdly prepared for anything. She understood that if she wanted to perform, she must be prepared. It was what'd made her a good student and a good Girl Scout. Working on the fly wasn't her forte.

Everyone was counting on her to get them out of there. The burden bore down on Laci, like wearing three of her backpacks. She sat on the dry grass, opened the journal, balanced the jewel within the outline, and focused on the passage again. Buzz closed his eyes tightly, getting ready to take the swirling trip, but nothing happened.

"Nothing's happening. You did something wrong," Ethan accused her.

Penny instinctively jumped to Laci's defense. "Don't blame her. She's the only one of us smart enough to get us out of here."

"No, she's the one who got us into this mess with all her book-reading-dragon-loving-magic-chanting-time-warping stuff," Ethan responded.

"I didn't mean to," Laci whispered to herself. "That should have worked. Why didn't it work?" She flipped through the pages. One by one, she scanned each carefully and quickly.

"Hurry up!" Buzz complained as the dragon continued to wrap itself around his leg. Buzz tried to shake it off. "Go home to your momma."

"I've got an idea, Buzz." Ethan looked around and found a stick. "Here you go, little dragon. Fetch!" He threw the stick with all his might down the side of the knoll. The baby dragon followed the stick in the air with its eyes. There appeared to be a grin on its face with its mouth open wide as if it were smiling. Suddenly it ran, but not to fetch the stick; instead, it jumped on Ethan's leg.

Buzz laughed. "That's the best idea you've ever had."

Ethan tried to shake the dragon free of his leg. The sight of Ethan doing this strange hopping dance with the dragon attached to his leg broke the tension, and Penny joined in with Buzz, laughing at Ethan.

Finally, Ethan could no longer keep the grimace on his face, and he cracked up, too. Looking at her three friends, who were almost in tears, Laci also began to laugh; however, the fun came to an abrupt end when Penny noticed something in the sky.

"Hey, guys, what's that?" she asked as she pointed.

Far off, in the distant sky, loomed a dark figure that appeared to be headed their way. "Maybe it's just a big bird," said Buzz.

"No bird is that big," said Laci.

"Is it a plane?" asked Ethan.

"It's Superman," Penny mumbled under her breath.

"I know what that is," said Laci, frozen in her tracks.

"I think you're right," said Penny, taking control. "We need to run. NOW!"

Coming into view at a rapid pace was a magnificent but decidedly lethal dragon. Its underbelly was a majestic metallic gold that appeared to be illuminated from beneath its skin. Its head was black and narrow with hints of red around its mouth. On the side of its head were two large horns that seemed to start where the ears should have been but extended high above the dragon's brow. Two smaller horns adorned the center of its head. Huge spikes protruded from the chest right at the point where its arms and wings connected to its body. The metallic gold continued on the underside of its wings and was almost blinding when the sun reflected off them. The long tail was adorned with a spiked lance that was, no doubt, used for battle and not just ornamental.

The speed at which it traveled was astonishing. For something that seemed so far away just a few seconds ago, it was rapidly closing in on them.

"Head for the trees!" yelled Penny as she led them down the knoll to the edge of the woodland. The boys were right behind her, but Laci was lagging, trying to run down the hill with her heavy backpack slapping against her side.

"Laci, duck!" screamed Ethan.

Laci dove to the ground, sliding partially down the hill just as the dragon swooped over her then back up high into the sky.

Laci scrambled to her feet, her heart pounding. "Please don't kill me, please don't kill me. I mean you no harm." She repeated her mantra until she reached the others in the safety of the forest.

Hiding among the enormous trees, the four of them searched the sky for any sign of the dragon. "I don't think it can see us under these trees," said Ethan.

"Until it burns them down," added Buzz.

"Buzz has a point," said Penny. "Let's work our way through using them for cover and try and get down to that village we saw." Still trying to catch their breath, they all agreed with the plan and kept moving.

They reached the end of the wooded area and saw a small shed about twenty yards away across an open grassy area. "I say we make a run for it to that building," said Ethan.

Nodding, Penny said, "I agree."

Before the other two could say a word, Penny and Ethan were in a full sprint to the shed. Penny reached the door first and threw it open. Ethan was right behind her and dove in. Buzz and Laci were running as fast as they could, but both were tired. Penny watched as the dark silhouette of the dragon covered her friends, giving them that extra motivation they needed to run faster. Laci made it to the door first, followed by Buzz, who tripped his way in. Penny quickly shut the door behind them.

It was dirty and dim inside the shed. There were double doors that opened in the front where they had entered and one small glass paned window on the side. The back corners were filled from dirty floor to ceiling with piles of split logs. They huddled down on the ground under the solitary window and looked up to see if they could tell what the dragon was doing.

"Now what do we do?" asked Ethan.

All three turned and stared at Laci.

"Seriously?" said Laci. "I read about them in books, but I've never been chased by one before. I'm a little freaked out, so don't look to me for answers right now. Just be quiet. We don't want it to hear us."

At this point, they were all a little freaked out.

Buzz broke the silence, "Oh no!" The others quickly shushed him. He emphatically pointed to the corner of the shed. "Look." In the corner of the woodshed, crawling toward Buzz out of the darkness was the baby dragon.

"How the heck did you beat us down here?" questioned Laci.

The closer it got to Buzz, the more Buzz tried to move away from it, but he was finding it hard to move in such tight quarters.

Penny shook her head. "I guess you're the mom again. Apparently Ethan is only stepmom or something."

Ethan corrected her, "Step-DAD."

Buzz crawled around the room, avoiding the dragon. The dragon then did something that took them all by surprise. It sat in the middle of the dirt floor and began to cry. It was a pathetic cry, like a sad toddler who'd lost his ball down the sewer grate, but it had a seagull-screeching, ear-piercing quality to it and was about ten times louder. In unison, they shushed the dragon, but, since apparently the dragon didn't understand that English exclamation, it continued to whine. The woodshed was engulfed in shadows, indicating the big dragon could hear the cry. The wingspan was so vast that when it beat its wings, the air pushed down on the roof of the shed, causing dust and dirt to fall on them.

Knowing they needed to quiet the dragon, Penny ran to grab the baby, but it snapped at her. Her quick reflexes saved her hand and all ten fingers. She turned to Buzz. "Quiet that dragon or we are all dead." As she glared at him it wasn't obvious who Buzz was more afraid of: the fire breathing dragon outside or Penny.

Buzz moved closer to the baby dragon, and it immediately stopped crying, jumped up and down on Buzz's leg, and snuggled against him. Buzz reluctantly petted it like a dog, and within seconds, it was fast asleep. He looked proud of his accomplishment with a satisfied grin, waiting for their praise, which never came.

Suddenly, a gust of air rattled the shed, followed by a ground-shaking pulse. They looked around at each other, wondering what had just happened. Penny went to the door and peeked out. Terrified, she whispered to the others, "It's landed."

They could hear the deep breaths of the dragon as it passed by the shed. They crouched motionless under the window with their backs pressed against the wall. Not only did they hear it sniffing the ground and the walls, but that familiar methane smell was overwhelming. It rounded the side and approached the woodshed doors.

Buzz mouthed a jumbled Hail Mary while attempting, but failing to make the sign of the cross.

A loud screech in the distance startled them out of their silent formation and Buzz's haphazard prayer. The dragon pushed off the ground with its massive legs and flew away, back in the direction of the enormous mountain they had seen from the top of the knoll. It turned back once to circle the shed; then as quickly as it arrived, it vanished into the horizon behind the trees.

"It's gone, but we can't just sit here and wait for it to come back," Penny decided as she stood and brushed the dirt off of her pink dress.

"I agree," said Ethan.

Laci and Buzz nodded.

Penny continued, "I think our best bet is to head toward that little village. They obviously live with dragons, so they can probably tell us what to do with this one..." She pointed to the baby. "...and where to go to stay safe until we can figure out how to get home."

"We can't take Buzz's new child with us," Ethan said. "I mean, what if it starts crying again, and more big dragons come?"

"He's right," Laci admitted. "We have to keep the baby quiet or get away from it."

That gave Penny an idea. One by one, they quietly snuck out of the woodshed, leaving Buzz alone on the dirt floor with the sleeping baby on his lap.

Penny turned back to Buzz and whispered, "Now slowly pull your leg away from the baby without waking it."

Buzz started to pull his leg out, but his shoe got caught in the dragon's claws. He pulled harder, and his shoe popped off and hit the dragon on the head, coming to a rest there.

"Buzz, c'mon, leave your shoe," pleaded Penny.

"I'm not leaving my shoe," Buzz whispered and carefully reached over to lift his shoe off the dragon's head.

The baby began to stir, but Buzz petted it a few times on the head and softly sang a homemade lullaby. "Go to sleep, little dragon. Please don't wake up and kill us." He tiptoed out the door with his shoe, and Penny shut the door and closed the latch.

With her back against the secured shed door, she said, "Well, unless he can figure out how to work a handle, I don't think he can get out right away."

Happy to have separated themselves from the baby, they quickly walked in the direction of the village.

"I kind of miss him." Buzz immediately broke the silence.

The response from the rest of the group was not positive.

Laci finally admitted, "Yeah, I miss him, too."

From behind, they heard a rustling coming from the shed. Buzz looked back. "I think he's awake." They started to walk faster toward the village.

"Well, it's going to take him a while to figure out how to get out of that shed," said a confident Ethan.

Then they heard that familiar sound of the baby dragon sneezing. A huge fireball came flying through one of the doors. The baby stepped through the hole, shook itself off, and looked around. As soon as it saw Buzz, it hopped in the air and sprinted down the hill to catch up.

Buzz looked at Penny. "Have you got a plan that could maybe keep the dragon away for say five minutes instead of thirty seconds?"

Penny didn't appreciate Buzz's sarcasm, and she stopped in her tracks.

Buzz looked like he realized he'd pushed his luck and started to backpedal. "I only meant, well, that two plans are better." He gave up speaking.

Looking beyond him, she spotted a small wooden wagon behind the shed, presumably for lugging the wood around. "Maybe we can keep him covered." She headed back up the hill, grabbed the wagon, and found an old horse blanket hanging on a hook inside the shed.

Buzz led the baby to where Penny was and, by patting the side, persuaded it to jump into the wagon. He gently put the blanket over the dragon and tucked it in, covering as far over the baby's head as possible to keep it out of sight. Ethan grabbed the handle and started to pull the wagon toward the village.

They headed down the only path they could find, which they correctly suspected would lead them to the village.

"What are we going to ask these people once we see them?" asked Ethan. *"Hi, can you direct us to the nearest portal? I need to get home. It's meatloaf night tonight."*

The group failed to answer, mainly because they hadn't thought that far ahead yet. They were just glad to not be running from the bloodthirsty beast.

"Hey, slow down," a motherly Buzz complained. "You're making the ride too bumpy for Digger."

They all stopped. "We're not calling the dragon Digger," said Laci.

"Why not? Digger the Dragon sounds cool."

Ethan shook his head. "No."

"Whatever. Just slow down," said Buzz.

Ethan started to say something, but, while looking back at Buzz, he wasn't paying attention to where he was going and hit a large tree root, causing the wagon to bounce and the dusty old horse blanket to release a fine powdery cloud all over the baby. With one sneeze, the blanket was reduced to something resembling an odd-shaped scarf.

"Your plans really are good, Penny," Laci said, and the boys started laughing. Their laughter was interrupted when they reached the end of the woods and saw the village.

"We can't just walk into town with a dragon in a cart. I think we stand out enough already." Laci looked right at Penny, who was still wearing a now-filthy, poufy pink dress.

"Laci's right. We don't even know how friendly they'll be. Only two of us should go, and the other two should stay here with the baby."

They all agreed to Penny's plan. Clearly, Buzz needed to stay in the woods with the dragon, and Laci was the smartest, so it would be advantageous to have her go into the village.

That left Penny and Ethan, and she asked, "Well, what do you think?"

Ethan put his foot in his mouth. "Well, it could be dangerous, so I think a man should go and protect Laci."

With that, Penny shoved him down into a bush. "We wouldn't want baby Digger to miss its stepmom. You stay here. We'll come back for you as soon as we can." She and Laci walked toward the village.

The baby got restless just as they left and began to chew on Buzz's jeans.

Ethan called out, "Hey, Laci, what does your dragon-field-guide thingy say you're supposed to feed baby dragons?"

Calling back over her shoulder as they continued to walk, Laci said, "I don't know. It never mentioned that."

Ethan muttered, "Probably because the book is just a bunch of made-up garbage since dragons don't really exist."

Buzz picked some weed-looking flowers and stuffed them into the baby's face. The dragon sneezed and lit them on fire.

"Nope, not that," said Ethan.

CHAPTER TEN

As THE GIRLS ENTERED the village, it felt as if they were in a time warp. The dirt road wound down through the center of town. The buildings on either side were dark brown wooden structures, mostly built with logs or distressed wooden boards.

Laci, clearly not a fan of new situations, stuck close to Penny, though her eyes were repeatedly drawn sideways to the pink poufy dress that adorned her friend.

Penny caught this and looked down at the fluffy disaster she was wearing. It was bad enough when it had been clean, but portal travel wasn't advantageous to bridesmaid's dresses. "Maybe I'll blend in."

Laci nodded but then shook her head no.

"Well, do you think people in dragonland here will be wearing hoodies and Skechers instead?" Penny asked.

Laci took a quick inventory of her wardrobe. Her thin legs protruded straight out of her cut-off denim shorts. A blue short-sleeve t-shirt with a picture of a bunny on the front hung loosely on her small frame. Her ever-present, nondescript, blue hoodie was dirty but remained on her back. The only fashionable thing she had on was her pair of black Skechers, a hand-me-down from Penny. "I see your point," said Laci.

Just inside the village there appeared to be some sort of a small farmers market. "Maybe we can get something to eat. I'm starving," said Penny.

"I'm starving, too, but I don't think we have their kind of money."

"Probably not," admitted Penny. "We'll have to figure out something and get some food back to the boys. I'm sure they're as hungry as we are."

There were carts with food and wares parked in rows along the dirt road. They spotted a little girl no more than five years old, wandering around looking for her lost pets.

"Here kitty, kitty, kitty. Peaches! Fuzz Ball! Cupcake! Killer! Where are you?"

It was a sad sight. Both Laci and Penny slightly tilted their heads and let out an "Awwww" in unison. They quickly scanned their surroundings, but no kittens were in sight.

The drab brown dress the girl wore was torn and a few sizes too big for her. She would step on it accidentally every time she leaned forward to look under a cart for her missing companions.

Their attention was brought back to the task at hand when they felt the eyes of the village upon them. Not surprisingly, people weren't going out of their way to interact with the strangely dressed outsiders. Since it didn't appear anyone was going to stop and offer any assistance, Penny decided to ask one of them instead.

A woman was walking toward her. "Excuse me, ma'am, could you please help us?"

The woman said nothing but moved away from Penny as if she were a leper.

When that didn't work, Penny decided to approach someone from behind, giving them less of a chance to skirt around her. She tapped a man on the shoulder, who turned around and gasped, his eyes practically jumping out of his head. "Sorry to bother you, sir, but we were wondering where we are."

The man backed up, pointing at Penny. With a look of fear, the man repeated "Witch. You're a witch" as he quickly walked away.

The other villagers turned to see what the commotion was all about but eventually went back to their own business.

"It's just a bad bridesmaid's dress," Penny defended herself, but the man disappeared into a building.

"I'm getting the feeling that people around here are not very friendly." Laci stated the obvious.

"I'm beginning to believe the same thing," said Penny.

"Hey, Laci, take a look at that." Penny pointed to a building that had burned to the ground. Just one wall remained standing, and it was charred.

"Yeah, I noticed that, and that farmland on the backside of those buildings has been burned, too."

Penny looked between two buildings and could see the smoke rising from huge patches of ground that'd been torched but still had rows of fertile crops lining both sides of the scorched earth.

Laci stopped an old woman who was too slow and feeble to run from their questions. "Excuse me, ma'am, what happened to your village?"

She turned her weathered face toward the two girls and gave them a thorough once over. "Evil!" she snapped at them.

Penny was taken aback. She wondered if the old woman was talking about them, or what had done that to their village. "What's evil?" she asked.

"Evil has returned. The curse is back. The truce with the dragons is over. There will be dark days again. Dark days, I tell you." The old woman turned and shuffled away from them as quickly as she could, leaving Penny and Laci even more frightened at their situation than before.

From behind them they heard, "May I help you, ladies?"

Startled, they both whipped around to see the outline of a young man. The beams of the sun created an aura around him, blinding them slightly. As their eyes adjusted, they were left speechless at the sight of the Nordic eighteen-year-old demigod standing before them, who was, in fact, real. He was slightly more than six feet tall, dressed mostly in dark leather, with an off-white peasant shirt billowing around his muscular chest. His thick blond hair was gently tussled by the breeze and passed back and forth over one of his brilliant blue eyes.

Penny and Laci tried to get their mouths to work, but nothing came out.

"Are you two ladies all right?" he asked.

Penny managed to get out a breathy, "Yes." She shook her head as if coming out of a trance. "I mean, no, we aren't all right."

The young man moved closer to them, which made her heart beat faster.

"Well, then, how may I be of assistance to you?"

Penny glanced at Laci, who stood with her mouth agape. His physical presence was overwhelming her friend, so she gave her a slight shove.

"Well, um, you can help us." Penny returned her attention to him and clumsily started explaining. "We're lost and not sure where we are or how to get back, and that's just the beginning of our problems."

He politely tried to help. "Well, I know these lands very well. Why don't you tell me where you are from, and I am sure I can help you find your way home."

Penny snickered like she knew an inside joke. "Yeah, it's not that simple, but let's give it a try. We are from Midville. My name is Penny, and my talkative friend over here is Laci, and we appreciate any help you can give us."

"Midville?" The young man thought about it for a few seconds. "I'm not familiar with that land. Does it lie this side of Storgoteborg?"

"Lie this side of what?" Penny said, knowing that the chances of him helping them were the longest of long shots. "Well, could you tell us where we are right now?"

"Of course. How rude of me. My name is Hallvard, and you are in my village, Botkyrka."

Laci finally managed to speak, but all that came out was a muted "Monumental."

"I'm sorry, what did you say?" asked Hallvard.

"Don't worry about her. Can you tell me about the curse?" asked Penny.

"The curse? That's what some of the older villagers call it. They lived through much more turmoil than the younger kin."

Penny and Laci listened in complete rapture.

"It started at dawn when a Ravendrake came down out of the mountains. She scavenged and burned our village. We have lived in harmony with the dragons for the past twenty years, but suddenly we were attacked."

A disturbing thought occurred to Laci. "Did you say it just began?"

Hallvard turned his complete attention to her. "Yes, everything was quiet until earlier today. Why do you ask?"

Laci tried to lie, but it wasn't her best talent. "No reason, just trying to get all the facts."

Hallvard took this opportunity to give them a brief history of his village. "The time referred to as the Dark Days ended when I was a child. An evil, twin, shape-shifting dragon named Rau terrorized our lands, but he was destroyed, and, since then, the relationship between humans and dragons has been one of understanding. We do not enter their territory and they do not enter ours."

Laci looked a bit stunned that she was having a real conversation with a guy about dragons, and it was all authentic and factual. "So tell me more about Rau," she said.

"He was pure evil. Not only did he terrorize our land as well as those surrounding us, but he also managed dominance over the other dragons and manipulated them into attacking us. It was a bloody time." Hallvard choked up as he spoke. The wounds clearly ran deep.

Penny noticed and asked, "Are you okay? You don't have to talk about it if you don't want to."

Laci shot her a look that said *Would you shut up? Of course he has to talk about it.*

Hallvard lifted his head and continued. "It is okay. During that time is when I lost my father."

Penny felt badly. "I'm sorry, I didn't know."

"Do not be sorry. My father was a hero. He sacrificed his life so that others did not have to live in fear. If need be, I will do the same to stop this dragon from destroying our village."

"No!" Laci blurted out. Hallvard looked shocked by her concern, so she tried to cover it up by saying "I think we can figure out why this dragon has all of a sudden started attacking your village. And if we understand why, then maybe we can fix it."

Penny looked at Laci, knowing she had a pretty good idea as to why the dragon was attacking the village, wondering if she was about to divulge that information.

"I appreciate your concern, but I must do whatever it takes to protect my people, just like my father before me." Pride shone in his voice as he spoke about his father.

"Did your father die in battle like Beowulf?" Laci asked.

Penny was confused. "Who?"

Laci explained, "You know, with the dragons."

Penny looked at her as if she was from another planet.

Laci went on to explain. "Beowulf. He first defeated a monster called Grendel, and Grendel's mother, then he needed to defeat this fire drake dragon that was terrorizing Geatland. You know, his kingdom. He and his servants went to fight the dragon, but they lost, and only Beowulf and his faithful friend Wiglaf went to the dragon's lair to kill him. Together, they defeated the dragon, but Beowulf was mortally wounded and buried with the dragon's treasure."

"Nope. Doesn't ring a bell." Penny shook her head.

"Do you remember anything from lit class?"

Hallvard said, "You know the poem well. I'm impressed."

Laci blushed and squeaked out an inaudible respond.

"It is true that my father died fighting the dragons. Unfortunately, we were never able to find the body of Rau. Some say he was so badly wounded he went back to his secret lair and is still recovering to this day. Others say he flew so high trying to escape the fighting that he got trapped on the dark side of the moon."

Penny snickered but saw Laci was obviously enraptured with every word.

"All the men who fought then either died fighting the dragons or soon after from their wounds. Legends say one man survived, who now lives deep in the woods, but no one has seen him for years."

"I'd love to talk with him," Laci said.

"We don't have time to wander into the woods, Laci. We have our own problems to deal with," said Penny, who was more interested in getting home than listening to stories about a land she wanted to leave as soon as possible.

CHAPTER ELEVEN

A SCREECH FROM THE sky interrupted their history of Botkyrka lesson. The same dragon they had hidden from in the woodshed was back. Its golden underbelly and blue-black scales shimmered in the sunlight. It soared overhead and created a frightening shadow that covered half the village at once. Screaming villagers scattered and took shelter.

The little girl looked frightened but wouldn't give up looking for her kittens. She began to call frantically for them. Hallvard spotted the girl and swooped her up like a falcon grabbing a mouse. He swiftly returned her to her mother, who was running toward them.

"Quickly, get into your home!"

Penny and Laci watched in awe at the power and grace in which Hallvard moved. During the chaos, a thought came to both of them: the boys! They looked up in the sky and didn't see the dragon. Now was their chance. They headed out to the dirt road in a full sprint.

Hallvard saw the girls racing toward the forest and yelled, "Where are you going? It's not safe in the woods."

When the girls kept running without looking back, Hallvard chased after them. It didn't take long for him to catch up and ask, "Where are you going? Stay in the village, and I can protect you."

The girls were listening, but they continued running. They were almost to the spot where they had left Ethan and Buzz.

"We have something we need to check on," said Penny.

As they reached the secluded area, Ethan hushed them in a loud whisper, "He's sleeping!" He pointed to Buzz who was cradling the baby dragon as it slept on his lap. Buzz looked uncomfortable, as the baby dragon weighed almost as much as he did. Seeing the two boys with the baby, Hallvard came to an abrupt stop.

Ethan looked Hallvard up and down, mentally sizing up the perfect specimen to his comparatively puny body, then turned to Penny. "Where did you get Thor Jr.?"

Hallvard looked behind him to see who Ethan was talking about then realized he was referring to him. "My name is not Thor. It is Hallvard, and you are?"

Penny and Laci gazed at Hallvard and watched him in action.

Ethan, already exhibiting pangs of jealousy, ignored him.

The giant dragon screeched from above. Everyone except for Hallvard instinctively ducked. Hallvard focused on the baby dragon sitting in Buzz's lap. "Where did you get that dragon? And, more importantly, why do you possess that dragon?" Hallvard's expression showed how ignorant the boys with a baby dragon must be.

The angry dragon continued to circle above, looking down below through the trees. "If she finds us with her baby, she will kill us all."

"Her baby?" the boys yelled in unison.

The commotion woke little Digger, and it started to cry out.

"That's its mother?" Buzz jumped up and got away from Digger, scanning the sky for the mother, but the baby kept following him, making a small shriek each time it jumped up and down on his leg. Backing away from it, Buzz tripped over a clump of vines tangled around low-lying branches. He used his hands to push the baby away.

Hallvard yelled at Buzz. "Stop touching the baby! The mother will smell you on it and be able to track you down and kill you." Buzz continued to try to separate himself from the baby, but his efforts were in vain.

Hallvard looked around at all of them. "Why would you steal a baby dragon from its mother?"

The two boys looked to Penny and Laci to explain the story about how a mythical creature had appeared in the attic of Penny's grandma and how they had all been sucked into a portal and had landed there.

"So girls, do you want to explain it to him?" asked Ethan.

Before they could get a word out, the mother dragon caught sight of her baby with the humans and targeted them. Wings back, and now in a full dive mode, they only had seconds to react.

Hallvard spotted the silent approach and yelled, "Move!" He started running deeper into the woods.

They immediately chased him.

Coming down for the kill, her talons were stretched wide, but the group managed to stay under large trees and escaped being snapped up in her grip as she veered away to avoid entangling her wings in the branches. The baby was frightened by the mother's attack and followed Buzz. Mama ascended again, trying to locate the group.

Still on the run, Hallvard started to put the pieces together. "No wonder the mother has been terrorizing our village. She is looking for her baby."

Although Penny would have liked to stop and explain, there wasn't time.

Hallvard continued, "You are responsible for nearly destroying everything we have. How foolish can you be?"

Penny had had enough. No matter how good-looking, she wasn't going to take this from anyone. She grabbed Hallvard by the shoulder to slow him down. The group came to a stop in a heavily wooded area, the canopy of trees almost completely blocked out the sky. "We didn't steal anyone's baby! It came to us."

Hallvard looked deep into her eyes, which messed with Penny's concentration. "How does a dragon just come to you?"

Penny scrunched up her face, showing the pain of having to explain. "We're not quite sure."

Hallvard studied her, and she knew he believed she was telling the truth.

"So somehow the baby dragon ended up in your charge, and now my village is being destroyed as the mother searches for it?"

Penny was relieved. "Yes, and we are very sorry about your village, but we didn't steal it."

Laci jumped in. "Yes, we would never steal a dragon."

"It doesn't matter how you got it. What matters is the fact that we must return this baby to the dragon's lair," said Hallvard.

Buzz didn't look happy. "Dragon's lair sounds dangerous."

"We need to head to those mountains over there." Hallvard pointed toward the west. "That's where they live. We must move quickly to lead the mother away from my village."

Startlingly, a huge fireball erupted overhead and burned the greenery. They had to dodge the flames and burning patches of flora. Laci was hit by falling debris. Her backpack began to smoke. She stopped as the rest of them continued running. She threw her backpack onto the ground to put the fire out.

"Come on, Laci. Just leave it!" Ethan yelled to her. Of course, they all knew that Laci would never leave her backpack, and, considering it contained the journal, which appeared to be their only chance of ever getting back home, it would be best not to leave it in the forest.

Laci scrambled to her feet, and Hallvard was right in front of her with his hand outstretched to help her. "Don't fall behind. It could mean your death."

She threw the bag over her shoulder and raced to keep up with Hallvard and rejoin the group.

Once they were all together, Hallvard slowed the pace down and searched the sky for the dragon.

Ethan had a chance to recall what Hallvard had said earlier and questioned him. "Hey, you said *they*. Did you mean *they* as in the mother and baby, or did you mean other dragons?"

"They live in the mountains. All the dragons live there."

Ethan gulped as the realization hit him. "There are more?"

"There are many," Hallvard explained, "but we can find the cave where the baby belongs easily enough. It appears young enough to have a birthing chamber. However, if the mother has abandoned the chamber, we must climb to search for a dwelling with two piles of jewels."

"Jewels?" Penny perked up.

"Yes. Duck!" Hallvard pressed his hand on Penny's head, pushing her to the ground as another flame ball soared over them and hit the trees.

While lying there on the ground inches away from Hallvard's face, Penny joked, "Well, what is it, jewels or ducks?"

Laci butted in to the conversation. "Yes, of course, jewels. Other bedding is too flammable, in case they snore flames at night, so dragons prefer to sleep on a bed of jewels. Don't you remember? I read that earlier today." Laci brushed herself off as she got up.

Hallvard stood and smiled at her vast knowledge of dragons.

"Gee, Laci, when you rattled off 1001 dragon facts, I guess we lost track," Ethan muttered.

Hallvard intervened, "You would be wise to listen to this one, young man. She is full of knowledge." Hallvard smiled again at a blushing Laci. He gave her a light punch on the shoulder, knocking her back into motion.

Ethan displayed his unhappiness of being referred to as 'young man' by mocking under his breath, "Yeah, listening to her is what got us into this mess."

Now that the trees created a thick canopy, they could travel at a slower pace, knowing they were hidden from the dragon.

Hallvard asked, "Where are you from again? Where is this Midville you spoke of?"

They all looked at Laci, but Penny tried to help, "It's complicated."

"How can a place be complicated?" he questioned.

Penny laughed, recognizing his point. "Well, it's not just that we're from another land. We may be from… another time."

Hallvard stopped. "That does sound complicated."

Penny decided to spill the beans and tell him everything. She explained how they'd found the journal under the floorboards and how the dragon had appeared in her grandmother's attic, which was strange since they didn't have dragons where they came from. She told him how they'd opened the portal and had all got sucked in, how they'd landed just outside his village and then how they'd met him and ended up running from a fire-breathing dragon in the middle of the forest.

Hallvard looked like he wasn't sure if she was telling the truth or completely crazy. "I'm not certain what to make of your story, Penny, but I will help you and your friends get back home. However, we must first return the baby to its lair." He looked around the forest and spotted a narrow trail. "Come, follow me this way."

Since the rest of the group had no idea where to go, they followed him without reservation. This trail was thick with vegetation, which was a benefit for hiding from the dragon, but it dramatically slowed down their pace. Hallvard was strong enough to push through it without too much effort.

Penny and Ethan competed to see which of them could make it look easier, with their eyes darting back and forth, checking up on the other. Laci couldn't go two steps without her backpack getting caught on a tree branch or a vine, so she strapped it to her chest as a shield and lifted it occasionally to avoid getting branches in her face.

Buzz was struggling. His first priority was to shake the baby dragon off his pant leg, but that distracted him, and he ended up getting hit in the face with every other branch. He pleaded to his friends. "Guys, wait up!"

The dense forest gave way to a clearing. Hallvard raised his hand to stop the rest of the group from entering the open space. He stepped out alone and immediately the shadow of the dragon passed over them.

"Man, how did she find us?" asked Ethan.

"I told you, she is a hunter. She will not give up until she has her baby," Hallvard warned as he regained cover from the foliage.

"Well, then, let's just shove him out into this clearing and let his mom pick him up and take him home," Ethan suggested.

"Without the ability to fly, the baby is too small and vulnerable. Its mother would not be able to protect it from the myriad of viscous ground creatures lurking betwixt here and the caves, and she would seek revenge for its death. We must return the youngling to the safety of its birthing cave. Come, this way now." He moved on to another path, this one even more overgrown than the last one.

"But wait, if there are scary creatures that could kill Digger, what will they do to us?" Buzz shivered as he asked.

"You needn't fret over that now. We must press on."

They walked shielded from the sun by trees, but after about forty-five minutes, they found themselves back at the clearing. It appeared that they'd gone in a complete circle.

As delicately as she could put it, Penny asked, "Do you know where you're going?"

"Of course I do," Hallvard irritably responded, but the truth was, he was a bit lost. Although he'd envisioned himself as a great warrior, the village had been living peacefully since he was a boy. Without a father figure, he'd had no one to teach him how to truly lead. It was his first chance to prove himself and live up to his father's legacy. He picked a new path, and they continued onward.

After another thirty minutes, they were beginning to tire. "Maybe we can stop and ask for directions?" Ethan snarked.

Laci shot him a look of disapproval.

"I do not need directions!" Hallvard said as he indignantly pushed through a wall of vines and almost fell right off a cliff into the churning water of a river below. He teetered on the edge momentarily.

Quickly, he backed up, but as soon as he'd done this, Penny, who was not paying attention, bumped into him. Ethan bumped into her, Laci, then finally Buzz and the dragon. He started to lose his footing. Penny reached for him but missed. Knowing he was going over the cliff, he told them as quickly and as seriously as he could, "Now we take the river to wash the scent of the dragon off u-u-u-s-s-s-s-s-s..."

They looked over the cliff in horror. "Penny, did you just push Thor into the river? I think you killed him." Ethan peered down to see if Hallvard was now a floater or a swimmer.

"I didn't! You pushed me. It's your fault!"

"Hey, Laci pushed me." Ethan glanced back.

"I would never push him in!" exclaimed Laci.

"Uh, guys," Buzz interrupted, "I think he's waving for us to join him."

They all looked down to see Hallvard's head floating down the river, quite alive. They could barely make out what he was saying over the noise of the river.

"Yup, he wants us to follow him." Buzz didn't appear overly enthused about the prospect of jumping into the river.

Penny wasn't one to walk away from a challenge. "Okay. Let's do this." She looked directly at Ethan, daring him. She walked to the edge and jumped off. Ethan, his heart pounding, couldn't look chicken in front of Penny. He sucked in a deep breath and took the plunge.

Laci, Buzz, and the baby were left on the cliff. The two friends stared at each other for a moment in utter fear. "Let's go on the count of three," suggested Laci as she checked her backpack to make sure all the zippers were secured, and then tightened the straps around her.

"Okay, sounds good," agreed Buzz. A screech echoed from above. The two looked up to see a ball of flames headed straight for them.

"One, two, three!" They both said in rapid unison and leapt off the cliff. As they splashed down into the water, a few things were apparent: one, the water was freezing, snowpack run off, and chilling to the bone; two, Buzz was not a strong swimmer and struggled against the current; three, Laci's backpack weighed even more when wet. She battled to keep her head above water, but the pack kept dragging her under. They were both struggling too much to help the other as they were dragged down the fast-moving river.

Laci was losing strength fast. For her own survival, she should let go of the backpack, but she would never do that. She said to herself, *you can't drown. Everyone's counting on you to find a way home. Just hold on to it. We can't lose the journal. You'll find a way home.*

Buzz, on the other hand, was in full panic-mode. His arms were flailing, and he was yelling at the top of his lungs. "Help!" His cries were barely audible over the roar of the river.

The current pushed Laci a little closer to Buzz. She reached out to grab his hand. Buzz grasped for her; they saw in each other's faces what looked like the end. Suddenly, they felt themselves lifted out of the water. As their bodies hit the shoreline, Laci looked up to see Hallvard holding one of them in each hand. The sun shone down through his golden hair, making him look like an ancient God again. Laci was dazed and could only manage an anemic "Monumental" as he placed her gently onto the ground.

Buzz, on the other hand, jumped up and engulfed Hallvard in an enormous bear hug. "Dude, you are like the best guy ever! I thought I was a goner. You're like Superman, without the glasses and the cape and all. No wait, you're like Thor! Man, Ethan was right. You're just like Thor. All you need is the hammer. I love you, man."

Hallvard was slightly confused by Buzz's affection but gave him a reassuring pat on the back. "Let's get off the riverbank and out of sight. It's getting dark."

Penny was no worse for wear after her dip in the river and asked Hallvard, "You didn't plan that, did you?"

Hallvard looked at her. "Of course I planned it. I was looking for the river, and I found it."

Penny gave him a knowing smile, and Hallvard took the opportunity to change the subject.

"Everyone stay here." He climbed a small hill to see exactly where they were. In the distance, he could see the mountains where the dragons lived, but as for how to get there, he looked confused.

Then it happened, the worst possible thing imaginable, at least for Buzz. Digger crawled out of the river, cold and frightened, but when he saw Buzz, he filled with a renewed energy and happiness. As Buzz whimpered at the sight of Digger, Hallvard returned from his survey and saw the dragon bounding toward Buzz.

"You must break the bonds with this dragon. We jumped into the river to wash the scent off. Don't touch it."

It was too late; Digger had already attached itself to Buzz's leg.

"What do you want me to do? He loves me!" cried Buzz.

Hallvard shook his head in frustration. "We must find jarfalla leaves for both of you to sleep in, apart from each other. That will erase most of the scent."

Buzz looked defeated. "Couldn't we have done that instead of jumping off the cliff?"

They all turned to Hallvard for an answer.

"Jarfalla leaves will only do so much. We still needed the water." He didn't look completely sure of himself anymore. "We must get out of sight and find a place to sleep. The darkness will not stop her from hunting."

CHAPTER TWELVE

THE SUN WAS SETTING quickly behind the canopy of oversized trees, and with it, the temperature. Although she was too tough to admit it, Penny was shivering in the thin, wet, short-sleeve dress. She looked down at how torn and dirty it'd become, which wasn't surprising considering they'd been sucked through the vortex of Pixy Stix, chased by an angry dragon through the woods, washed down the rapids for about a mile, and dragged up onto the muddy shore. She hadn't liked the dress to begin with but felt terribly guilty now, looking at the irreparable damage. She could still hear her grandmother telling her to take it off just hours before as she'd run out the back door toward the garage.

Grandmother's house; what she wouldn't give to be back there right now. It was warm, clean, and had a comfortable bed to sleep in. *I can't think about sleep right now,* she thought to herself. She was so exhausted she found a huge rock and sat on it.

"Hallvard, what do we do now?" Penny asked.

He glanced over and noticed she was shivering uncontrollably. "We find shelter," he said as he took his brown leather jerkin off and put it over her shoulders.

It was wet and heavy now but was an instant relief from the cold. She thanked him, although she was a bit embarrassed for needing the help. She immediately felt badly after seeing Laci's face. Laci obviously liked and, more importantly, had something in common with Hallvard, but he had just exhibited chivalry toward Penny instead of Laci, as most boys did. Penny motioned for her to come over and huddle under the jerkin together. Laci and her chattering teeth rushed over to take up Penny's offer.

With all eyes on him, Hallvard made a decision. "We must head west toward the mountains. The sun will set in less than an hour, and we don't want to be unprotected." Hallvard was harboring a secret, one that he was desperate for the others not to find out; he was lost. He wasn't even sure if the dragon's lair they were looking for was actually in the western mountains. His father had been the village leader and a fearless dragon hunter, as was his father before him. If he could return the baby back to its mother to stop the carnage, the villagers would see him as a great leader like his father. Without hesitation, he headed west, or what he thought was west. With no reason to doubt him, the group blindly followed.

As they headed toward the sunset, they passed a giant feather-filled nest on the ground.

"Look." Hallvard pointed to the nest. "Those are Gullinkambi feathers, rather rare. Those were used to make the feather cloak worn by Freyja. It transformed her into a falcon so she could fly wherever she wanted."

Ethan looked at Buzz to initiate a mutual eye roll, but Buzz was already sucked into the story.

"Legend says that the goddess Frigg was the true owner of the cloak. Those feathers are hard to find. You are lucky to have seen them."

"Wow!" Buzz said as he picked one up.

"And legend says that anyone who touches one without Frigg's permission is subject to sudden death." Hallvard turned to look at Buzz, who froze in fear. "I am only kidding you about the sudden death punishment," Hallvard said.

"That's not funny. Why are you always mentioning death when you look at me?" asked a rattled Buzz.

Ethan laughed. "I thought it was funny."

"You can keep the feather," said Hallvard.

Buzz was about to break it in half and stuff it into his pocket when Laci ran over to rescue the feather. She quickly pulled it out of his hand and put it safely between the pages of a book in her backpack.

Laci looked at Hallvard and asked, "How did Frigg lose the coat to Freyja?"

"That's a good question, and, as with most stories that involve gods and goddesses, it is full of greed and trickery."

Laci's eyes widened.

"As I'm sure you know, Frigg was Odin's wife. And Freyja was the goddess of love... well, lust."

Laci looked down at the ground, allowing her wayward locks of hair to fall forward and cover up her flushed cheeks.

Hallvard smiled at her modesty and continued the story. "Frigg loved Brisingamen more than the cloak."

"What? Brings in men?" asked Buzz.

Hallvard laughed. "Brisingamen was a necklace made by the dwarfs. Not just any necklace, one of the most beautiful of all time."

Ethan scoffed.

"She wanted to buy it, but the dwarfs said no. She asked what the price, and they said she must spend the night with each of them."

"Aaahh gross, with the dwarfs?" said a repulsed Penny.

"Yes, with the dwarfs. After the four nights, they gave her the necklace, and she returned home. But Loki had followed her and told Odin what she had done."

Buzz looked confused. "Loki? You mean the bad guy?"

"Loki is a complicated one. Sometimes he assists the gods, and other times he causes them problems."

Ethan interrupted, "Wait, isn't Loki Thor's brother?"

"So you know the legends as well?" said Hallvard.

"He only knows that 'cuz he saw the movie," Buzz explained.

Hallvard looked confused.

"Never mind. Go on," said Ethan.

"Odin then told Loki to use his shape-shifting abilities to steal the necklace. Freyja knew it had been Loki who'd stolen the necklace and gone to Odin, but Odin told her that the only way she could ever see Brisingamen again was if she would create hatred among men and war without end. She agreed."

"That's a terrible thing to do," Ethan said.

"You'd be amazed what women will do for jewelry," Hallvard said as he bent down, grabbed at the stems, and tore out the most enormous leaves they'd ever seen.

"Are you making a dragon-sized salad?" Penny asked.

Hallvard laughed. "These are jarfalla leaves. There is also an interesting story about them."

Laci looked excited at the opportunity to hear another story. Hallvard was acutely aware that he could merely recite the alphabet to keep this sweet girl interested.

"One day a greedy mortal man prayed to the god Njord for riches. But Forseti, the god of justice, altered the riches. He filled the man's land with jarfalla leaves instead. The man became irate with the gods for tricking him. What he didn't know was the true value of these leaves. He died never knowing what gift was given to him."

Buzz grabbed one. "What are they made of, gold? No... silver! No... platinum, that's it, isn't it? Or maybe they have diamonds in them." He examined one closely, looking for miniature diamonds.

"Buzz, don't you listen? Hallvard just explained what they do. When we got out of the river, remember?" Laci said.

"No," Buzz answered honestly.

Hallvard shook his head. "There are no diamonds, but, for you especially, they are worth more than diamonds. They just might save your life." He had Buzz's complete attention. "By rubbing the leaves on yourself, you can hide from dragons. They can no longer smell your scent. It was how many survived the dark days." He handed Buzz several leaves.

"Does it really work?" Ethan asked.

Hallvard said quietly to Ethan, "We'll find out when that mother dragon catches up to us now, won't we?"

Ethan smiled.

"You're smiling 'cuz you know it works, right?" Buzz asked. "I mean, you've done this before, right? You're not just making this up so that I'll feel better about it. I'm not getting eaten by a dragon today, am I?"

Hallvard put a reassuring hand on his shoulder. "We shall do our best to prevent that." Hallvard came to an abrupt stop at the edge of the forest, which had quite a steep drop. He froze. This time they all kept a safe distance from the edge.

Since they'd stopped walking, Digger began to jump onto Buzz's leg again, so he smacked the baby dragon with his jarfalla leaves. "I don't want your mother to smell you on me, Digger. Get down!" Buzz was trying to be stern, but the big sad eyes staring back at him turned him to mush. "Aw, sorry, boy." Buzz and the dragon continued looking deep into each other's eyes until he was put into a trance by the dragon and passed out.

Once the group had slapped Buzz awake, their attention was drawn to the view. A vast valley lay in front of them. In the center of it was a castle that had been burned and crumbled to piles of grey stone rubble between towers and a broken drawbridge.

"Wow, that's so cool," Ethan said.

Hallvard stood in silence, staring at the debris.

"Hallvard, are you okay?" asked Laci.

He snapped out of it. "I am fine, but there is nothing for us here, and it is a treacherous journey through the valley. Many poisonous snakes, and if they don't get you, one of the underground traps will."

"Poisonous snakes, dragons, cliffs, and traps? Guessing this isn't a big tourist destination," Buzz scoffed.

"I bet this was beautiful at one time," said Laci.

"Very beautiful." Hallvard was glad that someone could see the beauty that once was. "This is a reminder of the dark days. This was a glorious kingdom until Rau came. Rau destroyed this kingdom and the family that ruled it. Crops were laid to waste, and a panic engulfed the villagers. Many men and wizards joined forces to defeat them, including my father. This is sacred ground now, because this is where Rau was stopped. My father fought honestly. However, the dragon did not, and my father died in this decisive battle. His body still lies in the castle."

With sadness in her voice Penny said, "I'm sorry. Losing a member of your family sucks."

Hallvard was unable to come up with any words.

They stood in silence until Buzz spoke. "Where's your mom?" he asked.

The others cringed.

Hallvard composed himself. "She died when I was seven. Even after the dragons were gone, distrust and suspicion persisted among the villagers. People were afraid they would return and that others were in league with the dragons and secretly working to bring them back."

"Sounds like a witch hunt," said Laci.

"That's exactly what it was, Miss Laci, and my mother was one of the innocent victims."

Ethan looked guilty. As tough as the last day has been for them, it was nothing compared to what that guy had lived through.

"Who raised you?" Buzz questioned.

Hallvard responded, "I raised myself."

CHAPTER THIRTEEN

THE SUN HAD ALMOST FINISHED setting, and it was getting extremely dark. Every little sound and broken twig underfoot made them jumpy. Penny turned to Laci, who was trying to stick close to Hallvard as he led them through the darkness. "I thought we were going to find shelter? These woods are endless."

Laci shrugged, not questioning Hallvard's leadership.

Little Digger started whimpering.

"Could you shut your kid up, Buzz? It's creeping me out." Ethan nervously glanced back at Buzz and his charge.

"Maybe his mom is nearby," Penny worried aloud.

"I hope not. I'm too tired to run like that again," Laci said as she glanced up to the sky.

Suddenly Hallvard stopped.

"Shhh!"

Everyone froze.

His eyes grew wide. "We are not alone." He crouched, put a dagger into the ground, and pressed his ear to it. "There's more than one."

"More than one? More than one what?" Buzz started to panic, and Digger jumped onto him, begging to be held. Without considering the consequences, Buzz picked him up with much difficulty. Realizing what he'd done, Buzz dropped Digger and rubbed the jarfalla leaves all over himself.

Hallvard stared at Buzz as if he'd lost his marbles. "Covering your scent right now is not going to help us."

"What will?" Penny asked in desperation.

"Run!"

"Oh, crap!" Laci said as she clutched the backpack to her chest.

They followed Hallvard as quickly as they could, not knowing what they were running from. Soon they heard heavy breathing and snorting. It began to close in on them. As usual, Laci was falling behind, and Buzz was in dead last. He slowed himself down further by looking behind him to identify the soon-to-be attackers.

His feet got tangled, and he tripped over Digger, who had decided to run underneath Buzz for protection. Buzz rolled to a dusty halt in a giant jarfalla plant. Digger was head-over-heels right along with him and ended up on his lap. As Buzz attempted to get up, he saw two enormous creatures charging toward him. They had the face and tusks of warthogs, the slanted back and spotted fur of hyenas, and tails like giant rats. The disgusting menagerie left Buzz motionless.

Like a watchdog, Digger ran and placed his stout body between Buzz and the surely rabid beasts.

"This would be a good time for your allergies, Digger," Buzz said. On cue, Digger sneezed, setting aflame the tuft of hair between the wild beady black eyes of the closest one.

Dazed and confused, the animal stumbled back, and rolled around on the ground until the flames burned out. Unfortunately, this seemed to make it angry, and the snarling became louder than before. Its determination was overwhelming as it ran full speed toward Digger. This time it easily pushed Digger aside with its huge skull and stopped just short of Buzz, baring fangs over his head. The drool, oozing down the sides of its mouth, began to drip.

Cowering in fear, Buzz curled up into a little ball, preparing for the end. "I'm so sorry for all the bad things I've ever done. I'm sorry for the time I put my dad's toothbrush in the toilet because he grounded me. I'm sorry that I put Vaseline on my sister's hairbrush, and she had to wash her hair like twenty times. I'm sorry that I told my little brother he was stupid. I'm sorry that I told my other little brother he was ugly. I'm sorry that I told my other little brother that he was — or was that my little sister? Oh wait, no, I told my sister she was ugly. Which one was it?"

"It's a stygg!" Hallvard came barreling out of the woods. He hurdled Buzz and the jarfalla bush like a gazelle, holding his knife high over his head, and landed on the creature. He impaled the beast in the middle of its ribcage. Sliding off the side, he ripped his blade up and over to the front of the doomed animal. It screamed in pain, wheezing until it dropped. Its partner paced back and forth, watching and snarling. Hallvard stood, bloody knife at the ready. He lunged toward the creature, and it retreated into the forest.

"It is frightened, but it will be back. We must find shelter quickly." He leaned over and extended a hand to Buzz.

"I think I love you."

"What?"

"Nothing."

Hallvard helped him out of the bush, and they quickly ran to catch up to the others.

Exhausted, hungry, and still a bit scared from the encounter with the stygg, the group continued to trudge through the forest.

Ethan turned to Penny. "I thought we were going to find shelter, not march around the forest forever."

Penny was about to respond when they came to another clearing, this one much smaller than the last.

In front of them stood a modest wooden structure. It had an A-frame roof, two windows in front, and a front door with a huge knocker on it. The grounds were fairly well kept, except for a large watermelon patch located in the front yard. Its placement was curious, but they were so tired and hungry, pleasant landscaping was the last thing on their minds.

"I guess this is our Holiday Inn," Penny said as she marched forward, over the watermelon patch, and reached for the knocker.

"Wait a minute!" Ethan ran over, grabbed her hand, and pulled it back. "We don't know what kind of weirdos live around here." He gazed over at Hallvard. "Let's take into consideration the fact that we are in the middle of nowhere. If it turns out Jack the Ripper lives here, no matter how much we scream, ain't nobody gonna help us."

"Ethan's right." Buzz nodded.

"But on the flipside, let's consider what the mama dragon could do to us. A lot more damage than a recluse wielding a knife," Laci said.

"Laci's right," Buzz agreed.

"Laci is correct. We will be safer inside the dwelling than we will be out in the open," Hallvard said.

Laci smiled.

"Hallvard's right," Buzz said.

"Oh, shut up, Buzz!" Penny yelled.

A black cat rounded the dwelling and walked up to them, rubbing against Laci's leg. As Laci bent down to pet the cat, Penny raised her hand again to grab the knocker. Before she could reach it, the door slowly opened, causing the cat to hiss and run off.

Standing in the doorway was a man, slightly hunched over with age. The dimly lit house behind him allowed enough illumination to reveal the stranger's dark hair, long limbs, and, though not overtly friendly, his large dark eyes had warmth to them. He peered at the bedraggled crew.

"What do you want?" he asked.

Penny began to speak, but Hallvard interrupted her. "Sorry to bother you at such an hour, sir. Allow me to introduce us. We are..." Hallvard paused. "...we are cold and hungry. An accident befell us at the river, and we are quite far from home at the moment without shelter or food. Could we beseech you to allow us to rest here for the night and possibly spare us a bit of food?"

The old man eyed them with a puzzled look and studied their strange clothing; especially Penny's ragged pink poufy disaster.

Penny noticed his long stare and perplexed look. Embarrassed beyond belief, she felt she should explain why she was wearing the dress, so as not to be confused for a witch again.

"I don't usually dress like this. I know it's hideous. I'd never wear it on purpose. You see, I was trying it on because somebody..." She glared in Laci's general direction. "...convinced me it was a good idea. Then the dragon, see, the dragon..." She pointed at little Digger who clutched Buzz's leg again. "...it appeared and we—"

Hallvard bumped into her to stop her exposition. "And we need to dry off and get a bit of nourishment and rest, if there is any possible way, kind sir."

The old man, who hadn't given any indication of his feeling toward their arrival at his door, looked down at the baby dragon again and up at Buzz, who had started petting Digger to calm him.

Buzz noticed the man staring at him and gave a toothy grin.

"So where did you acquire a baby dragon? They're so rare and worth a great deal of money. Don't you know it's not safe to be traveling with one?" the old man questioned.

Buzz said, "Well, he kind of came to us. You know, after Laci read that book." He had the old man's complete attention.

Penny realized that Buzz was saying too much, as usual, and jumped in. "Actually, we're bringing it back. Taking it back to its mother."

With the mention of the journal, Laci instinctively squeezed her backpack to her chest.

"That's a dangerous journey. Please come in, sit down by the fire, and get warm. I'll find you some blankets." He ushered them in and disappeared into the back, emerging just a few moments later with a stack of blankets.

They huddled by the fireplace to get warm and appreciatively accepted the woolen cloths.

The old man walked into the kitchen as the group examined their new surroundings.

"Everyone, stay here and please keep quiet," Hallvard said as he got up and exited the house.

"Where's he going?" a confused Buzz asked. "We finally have a chance to get warm, and he runs back out into the cold."

Laci looked concerned but was clearly too focused on getting warm to let it consume her.

The old man came back into the room and noticed Hallvard was gone. "Where's your companion?"

Buzz said, "He does that a lot, just runs off, or sometimes he runs back. Like just a bit ago, he ran back and saved me from those stygg things. He was awesome."

With reverence in his tone he said, "Yes, they can be nasty creatures if they feel threatened." The old man paused. "You never said where you hail from."

Penny, who had just been cut off by Hallvard, wasn't about to open up again, and Laci was just too darn shy.

Ethan looked to Penny as if he was asking permission to talk, but Buzz never asked anyone's permission before he opened his mouth. "Well, it's a funny story."

The old man looked at Buzz, intently waiting to hear the funny story. Buzz appeared to be slightly intimidated and stumbled for a second, but before he began speaking again, Hallvard returned with a handful of wet jarfalla leaves. Upon his entrance, the old man retreated to the kitchen.

"Here, let's lay these down so he has something to sleep on." Hallvard pointed at Digger.

"Shouldn't he sleep outside?" questioned Ethan.

"Too dangerous. If it starts to cry or its mother sees it, we could all be killed in our sleep. It is safer to keep him here with us, out of sight."

Buzz grabbed some leaves and started to lay them on the floor. "What if he has another allergy attack? I think he might. He smells even stronger than usual."

"I soaked them each in water to keep them moist enough to avoid any disasters of that nature," Hallvard explained.

"We seem to have enough disasters already. Thanks," Penny chimed in.

Buzz looked back toward the kitchen. "Well, he seems nice!"

Hallvard lowered his voice so only the group could hear. "I don't know who he is or what tribe he was originally from. I highly suggest that we give out as little information as possible to him. But it is too dangerous for us to be out now, so we shall stay here until dawn."

Penny sank down in embarrassment. She realized she'd probably said too much, all in an effort to clear up the reason for her unusual wardrobe. Laci reached over and squeezed her hand in encouragement. "Don't worry, he probably just thinks we're insane."

The old man returned with a plate of hot rolls and goat cheese.

"That looks delicious!" Ethan dug in.

"Thanks!" Buzz grabbed a handful of bread with one hand and with the other loaded up with cheese.

Hallvard looked to Penny and Laci and said, "Ladies first."

Ethan and Buzz both stopped momentarily but decided they were too hungry to care that they had been rude.

Both the girls delicately took a small portion of bread and cheese and passed it to Hallvard, who smiled and insisted they take more before he had any.

"You'll need your sleep. I'll leave you to get some. I hope these blankets will provide enough comfort for you," the old man said.

"Yes. Thank you. It is quite sufficient and generous of you," Hallvard assured him.

The old man left the room and blew out the oil lantern. The sound of a bolt sliding was heard as he locked the door to his bedroom.

The glow of the fire in the fireplace was still illuminating the room enough for them to see each other.

"I will stay awake and stand guard tonight. The rest of you get as much sleep as you can. We will leave at sunrise," Hallvard instructed. "Laci, where is that book?"

Laci glanced at Penny, who nodded, and then pointed to her backpack. "Good!"

Hallvard sat up and motioned for them all to lie down.

Laci silently reached into the backpack and slipped the jewel to Penny. Penny understood the secrecy and took it, hiding it in her combat boot. As much as they fought it, the day had been too long and exhausting. One by one, they all fell asleep.

CHAPTER FOURTEEN

SUNLIGHT HIT HALLVARD'S FACE, waking him from an unintentional sleep. As his eyes adjusted to the light, he saw the old man standing over Laci.

"Good morning!" Hallvard said loudly, causing everyone to wake up and the old man to jump back. "I would like to thank you for your hospitality before we depart, and it occurred to me that I never got your name. I am Hallvard of Botkyrka, and you are?"

The old man looked suspiciously about then introduced himself. "I am Thuban."

"Is that your first name or your last name?" Buzz asked. A playful Digger yawned as he woke up and jumped onto his lap.

"It is my only name," Thuban responded.

"Well, Thuban, we are greatly appreciative. We will fold up these blankets and be on our way now." Hallvard motioned for them to get up. As they did, he noticed Laci had slept on top of the backpack. She tried to work out the crick in her neck then discretely wiped the drool off her cheek as well as the backpack.

Penny patted down her boot to confirm the jewel was still in there, giving a nod to Laci. "Did you bring the hairbrush?" she asked.

Laci looked puzzled but then unzipped her backpack, spotted the journal, and responded with a nod.

"Good," Penny said as she jumped up to stand.

Buzz looked confused, which wasn't uncommon for him. "Don't you want to actually brush your hair?"

"Not necessarily. Just wanted to make sure we had one. Man, you know nothing about girls." Penny snapped the blanket straight and began to fold it quickly.

"She's right about that, Buzz," said Ethan.

Buzz nodded in agreement, as it was best not to question things he knew so little about.

Thuban left the room.

Penny motioned to Ethan and Buzz to fold their bedding. They moved too slowly for her liking, so she snatched the blankets away from the two boys, folded them quickly but neatly, and stacked them next to the fireplace. "All set to go." She moved to the door.

"You should have something to eat before we depart." Thuban entered with more rolls and goat cheese.

Penny shot a look to Hallvard then to Laci, who instinctively squeezed her backpack closer to her chest.

"Thank you for your kind offer, sir, but we can't ask you to join us. This is too dangerous," said Hallvard.

"You are but five children, and two of you are females. You won't survive without my help. This land is nothing like Botkyrka."

Penny stiffened at the *girls aren't as capable as boys* remark and was about to give him a piece of her mind when Hallvard, who had just been referred to as a child, responded. "With all due respect, sir, we have made it this far without anyone's help. We can handle it by ourselves."

Thuban packed up the rolls in a pouch. He turned to Ethan. "What would you do if a Chuvashia landed in front of you and began to stomp its front feet?"

Ethan looked at Hallvard for an answer but received none.

Thuban turned to Penny. "What would you do if a Ravendrake swooped down from overhead?"

She glared at him in defiance but knew they were in over their heads.

"If I don't take you there, you will all die. I cannot even guarantee your survival if I escort you, not all of you." He looked at Buzz.

Hallvard was about to protest, but Thuban cut him off. "I have lived among the dragons long enough to know their nature. They are to be both respected and feared. During the Dark Days, my brother was killed. I know how deadly dragons can be. That baby has to be taken back to its lair because its mother will find her baby eventually and require penance."

"What kind of penance?" Buzz asked with a gulp.

"She will eat one, if not all of you, and since you have brought the baby into my home, the scent is here, and she may choose to take retribution out on me, as well." Thuban moved his gaze to Hallvard.

Defeated, Hallvard accepted Thuban's offer and exited the front door.

"So, uh, what do you do if a Chu-va-lupa-thing stomps its feet?" Buzz asked Thuban.

"Let's hope you don't have to find out," Thuban responded as he grabbed his long overcoat and headed out the door.

Penny and Laci exited the house, talking under their breath to each other. "I'm not sure I trust him completely, but I think we have a better chance of surviving if he goes along," whispered Penny.

"I suppose. He does seem to know a lot about dragons," replied Laci.

Buzz tripped on one of the vines blocking the front path. "Why do you have all these vines in the walkway? You should really clean this up. Someone could trip — Well, see what I mean? Wait, are these? Oh my goodness, watermelon. I love watermelon. Can we take one along?" Without waiting for a response, Buzz clumsily picked one up and tried to carry it, but it fell and broke wide open.

Digger ran over and gobbled it up. He shouted to them down the path. "Hey, Laci, dragons eat watermelon!" She gave a thumbs-up without looking back. Buzz rushed to catch up to them with Digger close on his heels.

With Thuban leading the way, they headed toward the mountain dotted with caves that looked like tiny specs in the distance. Buzz wrapped jarfalla leaves around his hands like mittens, regularly pushing Digger off him and glancing constantly at the sky. The tension among the group increased, even more than after they'd fallen off the cliff into the raging river.

Hallvard broke the silence with another story. Whether it was to ease the tensions or show Thuban that he was knowledgeable about the land, only he knew. Positioning himself next to Laci he said, "You will find this interesting."

Laci looked up at him pondering how he could give her a recipe for goat-head soup, and she would find it interesting.

"This mountain we are headed to has many mysteries. On the west side is believed to be the giant ash tree, known as the World Tree, Yggdrasill. Below the tree, deep in the earth, is the Well of Wisdom, which is guarded by the giant Mimir. Many people have gone looking for this well and have never returned. Some people think Rau got his power and wisdom from defeating Mimir and drinking from the well."

Laci was mesmerized.

"But I don't believe that. If he had been wise, he would not have ruined the land."

Thuban glanced back with a muffled laugh.

Hallvard clearly didn't appreciate Thuban's lack of enthusiasm for his story but saw Laci was drinking in every word.

Before Hallvard could start another story, Buzz said, "I'm hungry." A chorus of "Me, too" came from the rest of the group.

"There is a village not too far from here where we can get something to eat," said Thuban.

"I don't know, the last time we went to a village, they weren't exactly excited to see us," said Penny.

"I'm sure they will like you even less where we are headed," quipped Thuban.

The group continued through the forest, following Thuban's lead and checking overhead constantly to see if the mother dragon was still tracking them but saw no sign of her.

Soon they found themselves at the edge of a clearing with a small village. It was smaller and more unsavory than Botkyrka. They instinctively moved closer together as they entered.

"Now, stay close to me and keep your mouths shut. This isn't the kind of place you want to draw attention," cautioned Thuban.

"Mom!" yelled Buzz, who'd apparently forgotten the warning he'd just been given. They all turned to shut him up. "But look." Buzz pointed to the woman who shared a striking resemblance with his mother.

The woman looked over at the strangers entering the town but went back to hanging her laundry when she didn't recognize any of them.

"You really think that your mom was going to be here, doing laundry?" Ethan asked as Buzz dejectedly kicked at the dirt.

"Won't they think it's strange we have a dragon with us?" Penny asked Hallvard.

Thuban answered. "She's right. I almost forgot he was with us. We need to leave the dragon on the outskirts of the village." He pointed to Buzz. "Take him about one-hundred paces back into the woods, and we will bring you something to eat."

Buzz nervously looked at him. "Alone?"

Thuban nodded, and Buzz reluctantly retreated with Digger back into the woods.

"You have a dragon with you. He's going to protect you better than we can," Ethan called out to him.

As they walked through the village, the idea of staying in the woods like a sitting duck for another stygg was actually more appealing. A group of men about forty yards ahead sharpened their collection of assorted blades. This wouldn't have been startling if they were in a blacksmith shop or appeared to be doing it as a form of employment. It wasn't the lack of various teeth in their menacing smiles that rattled the group as they passed by, but rather that the remaining teeth were all black. One of the dirty and, now as they got closer, quite smelly men licked his blade with his tongue as he stared unblinkingly at Ethan.

"Who are they?" Laci whispered to Hallvard.

"Bad men" was all Hallvard could manage to say.

"They are jewel pirates," Thuban quietly explained. "They wander through the villages outside the dragon caves, waiting for the right moment to move in and steal jewels from the dragons' lairs. When they fail to get into the caves, they pillage and plunder the villages in the interim. Few of them are successful in retrieving jewels from the caves, but those who do are wealthy beyond belief."

"Though even if they make it out of the caves with the jewels, they are hunted down by the dragons," said Hallvard, interjecting his own knowledge of the dragons.

"Yes, if you are going to steal from someone, it shouldn't be someone who breathes fire," jibed Thuban. This made Penny smile, which was all the encouragement the pirates needed as the path forced the group to walk directly past them.

"Ah, a fair maiden! Come be my wife!" The shortest, one-eyed, and possibly the smelliest of the pirates, grabbed Penny's arm and pulled her toward him. He was strong and pressed his body against hers, trying to kiss her, but Penny was a fighter and kicked him hard in the shin, which broke his grasp of her. Seizing the opportunity, she threw a right hook, connecting with his jaw, but unfortunately hurt her hand more than his face. Furious, he lunged again, getting a much stronger hold on her.

"You're going to pay for that," said the irate pirate. As he pulled her to him, he froze as the blade of a sword now pressed against his throat. Following the blade to the handle, he saw Thuban at the other end. Behind him, Hallvard eventually got his dagger unsheathed.

"I highly suggest you let her go immediately," said a calm and cool Thuban, who moved a lot more quickly than his age would suggest.

The pirate slowly loosened his grip on her, and she pulled away. "She's too small anyhow."

The others laughed, glaring at the group as they continued into the village.

Appreciatively, Penny walked next to Thuban. "So, do you always keep that in your coat?" she asked, but he didn't answer her as he led them deeper into town, his eyes darting in every direction, searching for more trouble.

"Well, thanks," she said quietly when she realized he was focused at the task at hand, and since that task was to keep them alive, she let him concentrate.

Unlike Hallvard's village, there were no farmers-market-type stands in this place. Instead, the overpowering stench merely enhanced the rickety shacks posing as buildings of trade. As Thuban had predicted, the townsfolk responded to their presence even less enthusiastically than they had in Botkyrka. People didn't just run and hide from them but actively warned others of their approach, as well.

As they passed a woman cowering against the wall of a shop displaying a sign that was simply an axe dangling from chains, Laci noticed movement in the woman's skirt. A small child with smudged cheeks peeked out from the folds of his mother's dark and dusty patchwork skirt. Laci smiled and wiggled her fingers in a friendly hello. The mother yanked the child to get him away from Laci, sending him hurling into a row of axes, presumably for sale, lined up against the front wall of the building. As they crashed down on the cobblestone entrance, Laci turned to make sure the boy was okay, but Thuban grabbed her arm and jerked her forward.

"This way." Thuban led them into what could only be described as a dive tavern from hell. The filth on the tables and floor complimented the gloom that hung in the air but paled in comparison to the people inhabiting the various tables.

"Sit here." Thuban motioned for them to take a table off to the side and out of the way as he walked up and spoke to the bartender in hushed tones.

"I'm never complaining about Denny's again," said a nervous Penny.

Moments later, Thuban returned with bowls of grey gruel that smelled like the locker room after a football game.

"Eat," Thuban instructed.

Ethan turned up his nose. "Maybe I should have stayed in the woods with Buzz."

Laci stared at her full spoon. It was unclear which was worse, having to eat this or starve to death. She looked at Hallvard, who began to eat. He kept a straight face, so she gave it a try. After all, split-pea soup looked gross but tasted pretty good to her. The spoon passed her lips without touching. She bit down with her teeth and slid the spoon out of her mouth, letting the glob of *nourishment* drop onto her tongue. As she slowly began to chew, the taste of what could be a wheat product was immediately overwhelmed by a petroleum skunk-like manure flavor. To avoid throwing up, she swallowed quickly. Her eyes began to water.

She glanced at Penny and Ethan who seemed to be suffering as much as she was. Hallvard was manning his way through the bowl with little enthusiasm, but Thuban scraped the bottom of his bowl as he finished and looked at the rest.

"Come on, hurry up. We don't have time to sit and enjoy our meals."

Ethan whispered to Penny, "Is that what we're doing? Enjoying our meal?"

Thuban stood. "Let's go."

They reluctantly shoveled in as much as they could tolerate.

"What about Buzz?" Ethan asked.

"All I could get for him are these rolls. But he'll be fine." Thuban pocketed some fresh, baked rolls.

"I should have stayed with Buzz," Ethan muttered.

Cautiously passing the dagger-sharpening crew, they returned to the woods to get Buzz and Digger. Thuban stopped Hallvard at the edge. "You go on. We will catch up in a minute."

Penny and Laci looked at Hallvard with concern. He nodded for them to continue.

Thuban handed the rolls to Ethan. "Take these to the chatty one."

Ethan accepted them, and soon as Thuban's back was turned, he stuck one into his mouth and the rest in his pocket.

They arrived to find Buzz wasn't alone. He and another boy tossed a ball back and forth while Digger eagerly chased it. Ethan rolled his eyes. "Scary men licking daggers and gruel probably made from dead rats, or playing ball and eating fresh bread."

Ethan handed Buzz the bread, who eagerly gobbled it down. "This is delicious! Thanks."

At first glance, the little boy was a miniature version of Buzz. He not only looked like Buzz, but he acted and spoke like him, as well.

"Who's your new friend?" Penny asked. She couldn't believe a mini-Buzz existed in this realm.

"What's that smell?" Buzz gasped without answering her question.

"Oh, Penny was hugging a smelly pirate earlier," Ethan explained.

"I was not hugging him!"

"Whatever you want to call it."

"Could you stand back a little?" Buzz asked, pinching his nose shut with his fingers. Meanwhile, his new friend did the same.

Penny was highly irritated but could tell that everyone, even Laci, was in agreement. She smelled nasty now. Hanging her head and pursing her lips, she took ten large steps away from the others.

"Thanks," Laci sheepishly said.

This new mini-Buzz was such a close match to Buzz that unfortunately they even talked the same. "You guys should have been here," Buzz began. "Zebb came walking through the forest — Zebb's his name. Digger got all excited like he was seeing me come through the forest, and he ran over to him—"

Zebb continued. "Then he starts jumping up and down on me, then running over to Buzz, then back to me. He was so confused—"

Buzz took his turn. "He just kept running back and forth, then we started to throw the ball around, and he kept running back and forth chasing—"

This time it was Ethan who interrupted. "I think we got it. He ran back and forth."

"But that's not all," said Buzz. "I said hi, then he said hi, then I said I need to find some jarfalla leaves, and he said, I was just picking them —"

Zebb said, "I was just picking them, then I showed him where he could find them, so we picked some and made mittens out of them so the dragons can't pick up our scent."

Ethan and Laci stood dumbfounded at the bizarre scene playing out before them. After several more minutes of listening to Buzz and Zebb talk about their fun afternoon of dragons and jarfalla leaves, Penny took ten giant steps back into the circle, smell or no smell.

"Okay, enough. We have things to do, like return a baby dragon and get back home. I'm going to need time to get my dress drycleaned before the wedding now."

"Really? You're still planning to wear that?" Buzz looked at her, a little surprised.

"No! You idiot, I'm being sarcastic! But what does need to happen is you need to get up, and we need to get moving. And no, your new friend isn't coming with us."

Buzz's face dropped. It was obvious he wanted to bring Zebb along.

Penny turned to find Hallvard and Thuban. As she stormed off, she shouted over her shoulder, "Walk your new friend to the edge of the forest and come right back. Now!" The run-in with the pirate had Penny on edge.

Dragging their feet in the dirt, Buzz and Zebb chatted and walked slowly back to the edge of the village. Zebb lived in the house where Buzz had thought he'd seen his mom. "Hey, that's so crazy you live here."

"I know!"

"Your mom totally reminds me of mine!"

"And your mom— Well, I haven't met her." A sudden lull engulfed their non-stop conversation as they blankly stared at each other.

In accordance to Penny's instructions and her mood, Zebb walked to his house. Buzz waved bye and yelled, "Wish us luck in the dragon caves!"

This immediately got the attention of the pirates who'd accosted Penny earlier. Unaware of them, Buzz jogged back to meet the others in the woods.

CHAPTER FIFTEEN

THE GROUP PLODDED THROUGH another insanely dense bit of forest. Laci used her backpack once again to shield her face. Penny glanced over at her with an envious look. Thuban led them unfazed by the gnarly, snapping vines. Hallvard let out an occasional grunt of pain, which caused Ethan to smile even though he'd said "Ouch" countless times in the past fifteen minutes.

"I think this is more painful than lunch was," Ethan said.

"Yeah, I'm hungry again. Can we stop for more soon? Just thinking about that bread makes me happy." Buzz was daydreaming about food when Ethan let a branch go, nearly knocking Buzz over. "Hey! What was that for? Isn't there an easier way to get there?"

"The closer we get to the caves, the more natural protection we need. Unless you want to swim through a lake filled with lindworms, this is the best route," said Thuban.

Buzz looked at Hallvard for an explanation. "Worms don't sound so bad."

"Think of them as dragons that swim instead of fly," said Hallvard.

Buzz thought about it. "This forest is pretty this time of year."

As Laci's stomach reminded her of their meal, she started to sweat. Her small frame had never handled new foods well. She felt a sudden sharp pain in her gut and realized what that meant. With no convenient bathrooms in the woods, she was horrified to realize she'd need to get the gruel out of her system.

Thuban turned to check on the group as they trudged through the tangled plants. "What's wrong with you?" he snapped at Laci, in response to her looking flushed and slightly doubled over.

"Um, I uh, I have to go to the bathroom."

"Well go! And hurry up." Thuban pointed to a bush about ten yards away. Laci looked back and forth nervously for a more private spot, but didn't see one.

"Don't worry," Penny told her, "we won't look." Penny made all of them turn around, even Thuban.

Laci scrambled and crouched behind the bush.

There was a noise, then a smell.

Everyone froze, except for Digger, who bounded over to investigate the sound but quickly retreated.

"OH, GAWD! WHAT'S THAT HORRIBLE SMELL?" Buzz reeled and gagged over the stench.

Ethan caught a whiff and said, "It actually smells a little better now than when they served it to us."

As if this event wasn't humiliating enough for Laci, she realized it wasn't like home. "Um, are there any plants here that I can, you know, clean with?" she asked.

"Jarfalla are safe," Hallvard called back to her over his shoulder.

Looking around, she didn't see any. "A little help, please."

Penny glanced at Buzz. "Unwrap your hands and give her some."

Buzz pulled his hands in to protect his lifesaving gloves. "But I— No, I need them."

Penny showed no patience for Buzz. "She needs them more right now, Buzz. Do it." As always, Penny won the battle.

He handed them to her, and she brought them to Laci, her breath held and head turned as she approached the bush.

"Thank you," Laci whispered.

After surviving perhaps the most embarrassing thing that'd ever happened to her in her entire life, Laci returned to the group. Unfortunately, her stomach was still in pain, but if Thuban had been right, and there were more challenges ahead, she knew she'd better suck it up and deal with the discomfort. She returned to the group and marched off with the rest of them.

Thuban passed a berry bush and tore some off. "Chew on these elderberries for a while. It will help."

Laci looked to Hallvard for his approval, but he wasn't looking back at her. He was looking ahead and seemed deep in thought, focused and driven. She looked down at the berries in her hand. They resembled blueberries, only larger and darker in color. *Well, this can't be any worse than the grey slop that just burned through my system,* she thought as she popped one in her mouth and began to chew. Braced for an acrid blast, she was pleased to find they were sweet and enjoyable. She looked back to see if she could possibly grab an additional handful, but the group had pressed on, and the bushes were too far behind them now.

Glancing at the berries in her hand, Hallvard said, "You know that the Black Elder tree is sacred to the Moon Goddess, and these berries are referred to as the elixir bolus."

Laci felt her stomach flutter, not from lunch, but from the reticent bliss she felt listening to him tell stories.

The woods started to thin out, and their pace had picked up accordingly. Along the horizon, they saw the Yggdrasill tree. It was a magnificent sight, even from a distance, with its massive trunk and roots that spread in all directions, both on the surface and below ground. The canopy was so massive that its shadow would cover a city block.

"Wow, look at that tree," said Penny.

"I can see why the Well of Wisdom sprung there," said Laci.

Lost in the beauty of this majestic sight, Penny got her foot tangled in a vine. "Dang it!" she cried. She tried to get her foot out, but the more she moved, the more tangled her foot got.

The group, oblivious to her predicament, kept moving along, leaving her behind.

She called out, "Um, I'm kinda stuck here."

Hallvard rushed to her aid. "Hold still," he instructed as he cut the vine with his dagger.

"No!" Thuban tried to stop him, but it was too late. The vine started to bleed sap, a dark red, thick, sticky sap that looked like blood, but smelled like spoiled yogurt.

"My foot won't come out." Penny was pulling harder, but the vine tightened, and then more began climbing around her.

"You fool!" Thuban exclaimed as he pushed Hallvard out of the way. "You never cut through a fagerklokke vine. They are unforgiving."

"What the heck does that mean?" Buzz looked wide-eyed as he backed away from the moving vine. "And what's that smell? Laci?"

Thuban inspected the vine without touching it. "The fagerklokke vine has a mind of its own. It is extremely territorial and will strangle and kill anything that tries to pull it from the ground or harm it in any way."

Hallvard fumbled with childhood rhymes about the fagerklokke. "A knife to the brain makes it feel no pain. That's it," he exclaimed as he impulsively stabbed the root of the vine in an attempt to kill it. More of the flora blood flowed out over the ground and splattered onto Penny's legs. Suddenly, the vine flew up toward the sky, taking Penny with it. As she dangled upside-down, she began to scream. The vine tightened and was cutting off the circulation in her foot.

"Stop it!" Thuban yelled as he pushed Hallvard into a puddle of the red sappy goop.

"Take these two on ahead, away from here" He shoved Laci and Ethan toward Hallvard, who stood, trying to regain some composure. They were frozen, not wanting to abandon Penny. "NOW!" he yelled.

Hallvard angrily turned and led them off.

Buzz attempted to follow, but Thuban grabbed his collar. "Not you. I need you here." Thuban petted the baby dragon, which calmed Digger immediately. He coaxed him over and sat him under Penny. He grabbed Buzz. "I need you to do exactly as I instruct."

Buzz nodded.

He bent Buzz over Digger like a coffee table wrapped over a big log. Stepping on Buzz's back, he climbed up to reach the noose around Penny's foot. Working his hands between the vines and Penny's ankle, he slowly pulled the vines to free her. "Stay as still as you can. If the vines feel they are not threatened, they will release you."

Penny tried to stay calm, but the pain in her ankle was excruciating. She was also struggling to keep the pink mess of a dress out of her face and not show anyone her underwear.

As Thuban manipulated the vines, the jewel fell out of her boot and landed in a pile of leaves.

Without warning, Thuban freed Penny's leg, and she fell to the ground with a thud. Her leg right above the boot was cut, but she didn't have time to worry about that.

"Now run," Thuban said, but then pointed to the jewel. "Pick that up first."

Penny did and stuffed it back into her other boot. It was obvious Thuban had seen the jewel but didn't seem fazed.

"These plants are terrible," Buzz cried as he readjusted his neck after having a one-hundred-eighty-pound man dig his boots into his back for the past few minutes.

"Go, Buzz!" Penny yelled out as a vine moved toward them.

They scrambled to get up without tripping over any of the other vines that littered the ground. Thuban grabbed the back of Buzz's collar and tossed him away from an advancing vine. As the vines thinned out, they quickened their pace. Even Digger ran as fast as he had when the mama dragon was chasing them. That had only been yesterday, one day ago, but it already seemed like they'd been there forever.

CHAPTER SIXTEEN

BY MID-AFTERNOON, THEY FINALLY reached the Yggdrasill tree and weren't far from the mountain. Up close the tree was even more magnificent. Its towering branches and huge presence made them all stop and stare. The tree roots were four feet wide in places and rolled through the soil like giant snakes that seemed to have no end. Standing underneath made it impossible to determine the height.

"This tree is bigger than a football field!" Ethan stated in amazement as he gazed at the thick branches spreading out above him.

Laci picked up a few leaves that had landed on the ground and put them into her backpack.

The mountain, which lay just past the behemoth tree, was a majestic rocky structure with a pointy spire at the top and was riddled with holes. "What the heck are all those holes for? It looks like it has gophers," Buzz said.

"Those are dragon caves," Hallvard explained. "We will be going into one to return the baby."

"What? Can't we just leave him here and let him find his way home?" Buzz asked nervously.

"Buzz, the dang thing won't stop following you. We might even have to leave you in the cave with it so we can escape," Penny teased him.

Buzz's mouth dropped. "You're kidding, right?"

She was teasing, mainly to ease her own nerves, but even Laci, who had actually dreamed of seeing a dragon close up, exhibited apprehension about going into a dragon's lair now that it'd become a reality and not just a fantasy.

"What we must do now is find the birthing chamber." Hallvard began to hatch a plan.

"There are hundreds of caves up there. Are we gonna knock on every door and ask if they lost their baby?" Ethan joked, not exactly appearing ecstatic at the prospect of venturing into dragon caves.

Laci muttered quietly, "Maybe just put its face on the back of a milk carton and see who claims it."

"What did you say, Laci?" asked Hallvard.

"Nothing, just looking forward to hearing your plan of attack."

"She is a Ravendrake, and they always reside on the east side of the mountain," Thuban interjected. "Unfortunately, we are currently on the west side of the mountain, which means that we will either cross the caves of the Chuvashia on the north or the Hellblaze Wyverns on the south.

Penny raised her hand. "I vote for Chuvashia. They have less blaze and hell in their names."

Hallvard spoke up. "No, the most evil dragons that ever existed were shape-shifters, Chuvashia."

The disgust in his voice reminded Penny of the painful memory of his father's death.

"Penny is right. They are less aggressive, usually." Laci started to feel confident in her assessment of what she had read and the fact that she had recent, albeit limited, field training.

"The girls are correct. Traveling to the south is almost certain suicide. We will travel to the north," Thuban said.

Hallvard reluctantly agreed, and they headed north, through the Chuvashian territory.

Penny noticed his demeanor had changed. He appeared to be on a different mission, one of revenge.

The path along the north side of the mountain provided an advantageous route for hiding, due to the tall grass. Some dragons found this tall grass a fertile hunting ground because of all the animals that called it home, but for the group, it was the best camouflage they could find. They moved alongside and under as many of the sparsely scattered trees as possible, so as not to be visible from the air.

Penny pulled her torn skirt up a bit and looked at her wound. It sent stinging pains up her leg that traveled through her entire body as if moving through her bloodstream. To relieve her anxiety, she ran ahead to Thuban for his opinion. In doing so, she passed Hallvard, but she had no time to worry about his feelings. "I got a nasty scratch from the vines, and it stings. Should I be chewing any berries or anything to make it feel better?" She pulled up the skirt to show him quickly as they maintained their brisk pace.

Thuban took a brief glance at it. "You will be fine. You should wash it so it doesn't become infected. Then you can wrap it in mjodurt." Thuban walked ahead, but Penny was still anxious.

Hallvard moved next to her. "Don't worry, I will help you take care of it."

Hallvard's concern made Penny feel slightly better.

Laci, who was currently fighting a second wave of the stomach pains, was looking around for a bush to hide behind and glancing at Buzz's hands to see if he had more of those leaves, when she noticed movement behind them. "I think I just saw something."

Hallvard pulled out his dagger. "Where?"

"She's right. We are not alone." Thuban sniffed the air and slowly drew his sword.

"The grass. It's moving!" Buzz yelled and pointed. They instinctively formed a circle with their backs to each other as they scanned every direction. The grass flattened in one area and then another, but none of them could see exactly what was causing it.

"One thing is for sure. It's either very fast, or there's more than one," Penny said as she grabbed Laci's hand.

"This is like Jurassic Park! A pack of velociraptors is gonna eat us, isn't it?" cried Buzz.

"A pack of what?" asked Hallvard.

Thuban ignored Buzz and stayed focused on the advancing predators.

"Oh, never mind," Buzz said. "I forgot dinosaurs aren't real." He looked down at Digger at his feet. "Are they?"

Their pursuer systematically moved closer and closer.

"I think we should run," Penny said.

Hallvard nodded, as did Thuban, and the group took off through the high grass. As a result, they stopped utilizing the safety of the trees from predators in the sky.

Naturally, Buzz was in the rear. He kept looking back and saw the attackers spread out, encircling them. Finding that extra gear, he put on the speed. "I'm not getting eaten today," he said as he passed Ethan and caught up to Hallvard.

Ethan, now in the rear, caught a glimpse of what was chasing them and screamed out, "PIRATES!"

As soon as he'd yelled, one pirate jumped out at Hallvard and attached himself to his back, like Yoda on Luke.

The short, one-eyed, smelliest one jumped out and grabbed Penny, dragging her to the ground, rolling her away from the others.

"Not you again!" Penny slugged his jaw, which seemed to have slightly more of an effect than her earlier skirmish with him had.

He shook his head to clear it and grabbed her long blond hair, pulling her head back toward him. Then he wrapped his big hairy arm around her, pinning her arms to her sides. "You're going to have to do better than that, little girl."

Wriggling her right arm out of his grasp, she reached around and grabbed at his face. Getting a firm hold, she dug her nails in, and he screamed out in pain. Penny tightened her grip even more.

The smelly pirate continued yelling and dropped to his knees. Amazed at her strength over him, the weight of his dumpy little body broke her grasp as he hit the ground. There were lacerations on his face where her fingers had dug in.

She looked down at her arm, wondering where that strength and length had come from. With Penny distracted, the smelly man stumbled backward, retreated, and disappeared through the tall grass.

Meanwhile, Hallvard attempted to stab the black-toothed menace on his back with his dagger. "Get off me, you vile creature!" he said while trying to strike the pirate, but missed his mark every time.

The pirate was about to administer a lethal blow to Hallvard's neck with his own dagger when Laci raced over and clobbered the pirate in the head with her backpack. He fell to the ground, unconscious.

Amazed, Hallvard looked down at the pirate then over at tiny Laci and her giant backpack. "Thank you," he said to her with a smile.

"No problem."

"I think there were three of them. We must find the others." He ran to where he'd last seen Ethan, Buzz, and Thuban.

Penny appeared through the tall grass, and she and Laci followed the fast-moving Hallvard.

Moments later, the trio found Ethan and Buzz standing in a section of tall grass that'd been pushed down.

"Where's Thuban?" asked Hallvard.

"He and the huge pirate were battling it out with their swords, and they headed that way."

Before Ethan finished pointing, Hallvard was in full sprint. Over his shoulder he yelled, "Stay there. I will come back for you." He disappeared into the tall grass.

Buzz hugged Digger, not showing any concern about dragon scent at the moment, and Ethan and Penny shared a look of temporary relief.

Following the flattened grass path, Hallvard arrived to witness the pirate plunging his sword into Thuban's chest, but somehow, he had the strength to strike back. Both bodies dropped to the ground. Thuban slowly rose. Hallvard ran to help him to his feet. He pushed his arm away and stood on his own. Blood soaked through his shirt.

"We must get you to the village where we can get some help," Hallvard said.

Thuban pulled his sword out of the dead pirate lying on the ground and said, "Let's go. We are too exposed out here in the open. Are the children still alive?"

A stunned Hallvard replied, "They're fine, but what about you? You were stabbed. You're bleeding!"

"I am fine," Thuban said. "Where are the children?"

"But the b-blood—" Hallvard stuttered.

Thuban looked down at his blood-drenched shirt. "It's his blood." He pointed to the dead pirate on the ground. "Come on." He spotted the others and headed toward them.

A confused Hallvard followed.

Stunned by the amount of blood on his shirt, Penny started to ask, "Are you—"

Thuban cut her off. "I'm fine. There were three. I disposed of one. What happened to the other two?"

Ethan and Buzz looked at Penny, who explained, "Well the one-eyed smelly guy who wanted me as his wife earlier didn't like the way I grabbed his face and ran off." She looked down at her hand and arm, which appeared to be quite normal, and decided that this wasn't the right time or place to discuss her newfound strength, or whatever it was that had happened.

"Laci knocked out the other one with her backpack. She was extremely brave," said Hallvard.

"Way to go, Laci," Buzz said.

"That means you failed to eliminate the other two. We must keep moving." Thuban turned and resumed their trek toward the mountain.

CHAPTER SEVENTEEN

THE SUN WAS STILL out, but it wasn't apparent at the base of the mountain. A strange fog covered the ground, so they pressed themselves low and flat against the mountain to avoid being detected. The fog made it difficult to see, and they bumped into each other in the dizzying haze.

"Where did this fog come from?" asked Ethan.

"It is not fog," replied Hallvard. "It is dragons' breath."

"Can we maybe rest a little?" Penny asked, looking at her friends who appeared as scared, exhausted, and hungry as she was.

Laci, particularly, looked a little green, and Penny knew her best friend needed rest more than the others.

"For just a moment," Thuban reluctantly agreed.

"What time is it anyhow?" Buzz asked Thuban.

He and Hallvard both strained to locate the sun through the mist as Ethan reached into his pocket and pulled out a Ziploc bag with his iPhone in it. He held the phone into the air, trying to get even a single bar.

Buzz reached for the phone. "Oh, can I call my mom? She's gonna wonder where I am, and I don't want to get her mad at me 'cuz she'll ground me, then I won't be able to watch *Super Paranormal Facts* this week. It's gonna be a good episode too. There are some people who actually met Sasquatch. They live up in Washington State, and they were camping, and all of a sudden he shows up and sits next to them at their campfire, and they say he even drank a beer with them."

"I hope he didn't drive after that," Penny snidely said to Buzz, who appeared to be thinking about it and nodded.

"Didn't your phone get wrecked in the river?" Laci looked up from where she'd collapsed onto the ground.

"No, no, my mom gave me a waterproof case." Ethan held it up.

"That's a Ziploc!" Penny scoffed.

"It keeps the water out, okay?" Ethan continued trying desperately, but found no signal. It did, however, show him the time. "This is weird. It says it's four-thirty in the afternoon, but it's got yesterday's date. The last day of school was June 15, so today should be the 16th."

"Ethan, it's probably giving you the wrong date because it's a dinosaur of a phone. What is it, a hand-me-down from Fred Flintstone? That's generation one. They're on generation what, six now? I bet mine would get a signal here, if only it wasn't with my normal clothes." Penny sighed and looked at the filthy tattered and torn pink mess she was wearing.

"Time stopped. Maybe time stopped for us in our world, so no matter how long we're gone, they won't know." Laci thought aloud.

"Your world?" Thuban entered the conversation. "What do you mean by *your* world?"

Penny quickly covered. "Living in Midville feels like a whole 'nother world. Trust me," she said with a twang in her voice. "She just means it must have stopped when we left our area and fell into the river."

Thuban's face remained emotionless.

"May I see that?" Hallvard looked fascinated by the iPhone as Ethan handed it to him. "What does it do?"

"Uh, you call and text people, check your email, surf the web," Ethan said.

Looking puzzled, Hallvard asked, "Is it a weapon?" He pressed a few touchscreen buttons, pointing it away from him, but nothing happened.

"Only if you believe everything you read on the Internet. In that case, it can be dangerous," Laci explained, only further confusing Hallvard.

Thuban was busy fiddling with something in his coat pocket but kept glancing up to get a better look at the phone.

"Or if you write a text to a girl named Molly, and you really like her but accidentally press *Mom* and don't notice before you hit *Send*... That can get you grounded," Buzz added.

"You like Molly?" asked Ethan.

Buzz shrugged.

"It is approximately the same thickness as my blade. Can it slice?" Hallvard asked as he touched the metal edges.

Buzz was playing with Digger and started reciting the words to an infomercial for knives. "It slices, it dices, it chops it all up."

"Really?" Hallvard seemed intrigued and slammed an edge against the stem of a plant growing on the side of the mountain base.

"NO!" Ethan yelled as the phone face shattered into pieces. "You idiot! My phone!"

"But he said it would slice and dice, did he not?" Hallvard questioned.

"He's an idiot, too. Have you learned nothing?" Ethan mocked the way Hallvard spoke. "Give me that." He grabbed all the broken pieces and shoved them into his Ziploc.

"Maybe it can be fixed," Laci said encouragingly, but Ethan just shot her an angry look.

"I wonder if smashing it against a tree is covered under warranty?" joked Penny.

Ethan's anger prevented him from responding or even looking at her.

Thuban broke the short, uncomfortable silence. "Enough of this. We must keep moving." He showed no patience with the group. His earlier creepy-but-charming self had been displaced with a surly intolerance.

Hallvard responded by changing the subject and answering the question Buzz had posed earlier. "Buzz, you asked about the time. It is between None and Vespers."

"Say what?" Buzz asked.

"I said between None and Vespers," Hallvard repeated.

"He was asking what that meant," Laci politely explained. "We must use different words to describe the various times of day."

"I see. Well, None comes after Sext, which is when we consumed our mid-day meal." Hallvard explained, as Buzz's focus appeared to have shifted to those homemade rolls again. "Vespers is when the sun is setting on the horizon. At Compline it gets dark, and we will have to camp. We may not make it to the Ravendrake caves before dark."

Buzz gave him a blank stare. "When do we eat again?"

"We must keep moving. It is too dangerous to be on the ground after dark. Those pirates you failed to dispose of will still be following us, and the Vardo will be hunting," Thuban gruffly stated. He stopped searching his pockets and pulled out a pair of gloves then motioned for them to follow him.

"I probably don't want to know, but what are Vardo?" Penny asked.

"Witches," Laci whispered to her.

"Stop your talking. You will draw attention to us," Thuban snapped at them.

"Looks like somebody else's grey gruel isn't agreeing with them either," Penny whispered to Laci, who laughed as Penny rolled her eyes toward Thuban.

The first set of cave openings were referred to as the lower level. They were called that because they were almost accessible without having to climb at all — not that anyone would do that unless they had an overwhelming desire to be torched.

To avoid detection, Thuban went down on all fours and led them under the first few mouths of the caves. The smell of sulfur and rancid garbage filled the air.

Laci was next in line, scraping her knees constantly, but did her best to keep moving. The putrid mix of smells made her eyes water and didn't help her stomach problems or the headache she was developing.

Penny's dress tore a few more times. It was covered with dirt and mud, and now possibly dragon dung as well.

Buzz was crawling at eye-level with Digger, creating a stronger attachment, if possible. Ethan glanced over at them. "Please don't kiss the dragon. I can tell you want to."

"Don't—" Buzz responded, but in truth, he had grown overly attached to his little friend. Ethan grumbled something about his cell phone, though his most obvious problem was the proximity of his face to Digger's butt.

"Why does it smell so awful?" asked Penny when they were between caves.

"These are birthing chambers. The mothers give birth in the lower caves, providing a safe place for their young to learn to hunt," said a matter-of-fact Thuban. "The afterbirths are left for the baby to eat once it stops nursing, which can be several moons after their birth."

"As you know with Digger, baby dragons cannot fly. They need to be in caves close to the ground. Once they are able to fly, they will join the mother in her nest. Then someday, they will find a cave of their own," Hallvard elaborated.

"Not unlike humans," Laci added.

"Yeah, Laci, they're just like us," said Ethan.

"Freeze!" Hallvard said in a loud whisper. They all remained motionless, trying to make themselves invisible by pressing into the hard mountainside shrouded by the fog.

A Chuvashia dragon began to exit the cave they were directly under. It sniffed the air, then shook its head back and forth violently. Streams of what smelled like gasoline flew through the air and landed on them huddled underneath. It opened its wings that were so black they glowed blue. Then it let out a scream so piercing they had to cover their ears to prevent their eardrums from exploding.

"Monumental," Laci said as she peeked her head out of the ball she'd turned herself into. The dragon stepped to the edge of the cave, causing rocks to break off and fall on them huddled below. It turned its massive neck, twisted its head, let out another scream, and spotted them.

"Run!" Hallvard shouted. They stayed close to the side of the mountain, running as fast as they could. The commotion gained the attention of other dragons as well. Like back in Midville, once one dog barked, soon the whole neighborhood was barking. Only these *dogs* were giant and breathed fire.

"We're doooooomed!" Buzz yelled.

The dragon jumped down from her perch and stood behind them. No matter how fast they ran, they were no match for the dragons' speed. One stride and she was right behind Hallvard. She lunged at him, but he managed to avoid the bite; however, her huge head knocked him to the ground. Hallvard rolled on his back and drew his knife, posed, ready for battle.

The dragon hovered, preparing to devour him, but was knocked to the ground by another dragon that leapt out of her cave. That dragon was larger with dark red stripes on her back and several battle scars on her head. Hallvard seized the opportunity and ran. In a standoff, the two dragons circled each other in the tall grass. They exchanged bursts of fire, which had little effect on their tough exteriors. The battle-tested dragon leapt on top of the first, sinking her long teeth into her opponent's neck. Green blood oozed out of Hallvard's would-be attacker as it lay on the ground injured. Several more dragons flew out and began attacking the wounded dragon on the ground, tearing it apart like vultures, eating it alive.

The screams from the dragon were filled with pain, and although it had just tried to kill them, Penny felt sorry for it.

With the dragons in the immediate area behind them and preoccupied, they slowed their pace down from a sprint to nearly a stop to catch their breath.

"I need new underwear," Buzz said as he slammed his body into the side of the mountain base in exhaustion.

Laci fell to the ground, part from exhaustion, part in shock over what they'd just witnessed.

"No stopping. We must keep moving," Thuban told them.

"Hold on!" Doubled over, Buzz had trouble catching his breath.

"Can't we just rest for a minute?" pleaded Laci.

"Get up!" Thuban yelled at her.

Hallvard reached to help her up. "He's right. It's not safe here. We must keep moving." He put his arm around her to keep her moving, raising her adrenaline.

Crawling through the grass and rocks proved to be a slow form of travel. With nightfall rapidly approaching, they risked walking upright and only crouched when they went under the cave openings. After another hour of trudging through the landscape, they made it to the end of the north side where it began to turn to the east.

"We are close to the Ravendrake caves. We should start checking for the birthing cave. You go on to the next. We'll check here." Hallvard motioned for the others to go and grabbed Buzz boosting him up to peer into one that didn't appear occupied.

Buzz struggled to pull himself up, barely bringing his eyes over the edge. "Hey, there's a girl in there, way back in the corner. Hey. Lady! Lady!" Buzz started to wave at her, lost his balance, and stuck his sneaker in Hallvard's face.

"What are you doing?" an annoyed Hallvard asked.

The woman looked over and quickly grabbed a rock, which she painfully swallowed. Within a matter of seconds, she transformed into a Chuvashia.

"Oh no. Get me down! Get me down!" Buzz yelled as he frantically pumped his feet, causing them to crash to the ground.

The dragon rushed out to the edge of the cave, but Hallvard and Buzz remained out of sight under a nearby ledge. It flew off, giving the two an opportunity to catch up with the rest of the group.

"You guys, you missed the craziest thing ever. This lady in the cave ate a rock and turned into a dragon." Buzz was overwhelmed at the transformation and excitedly told the others.

"Have you been eating those leaves you keep wrapping around your hands? Because you sound crazy." Ethan stared at his hyperactive friend.

"Shape-shifters, the Chuvashia dragons, require a trigger to change their form," Hallvard explained. "Some need moonlight, some need to swallow a specific thing, like a rock, while others require water. There are many triggers. Some even require the presence of another. This happens rarely, mostly with twins. It is said that they lose their ability to return to their dragon form when they are unable to locate their trigger."

"Wow. I hope when it's time to go to the bathroom she's in dragon-form, or that's going to hurt!" Buzz cringed at the thought.

"Do you think this is funny?" a terse Thuban asked.

Buzz looked at him but didn't know what to say.

"That female you scared was sitting in a birthing chamber. By scaring her, you have disrupted her birthing cycle."

"I scared her? Did you see how big she got?" a confused Buzz asked.

Thuban walked toward him with anger in his eyes. "Yes, you scared her. As far as she knew, you were a pirate looking to steal her baby. You may not like them, but you had better start showing them some respect. Keep moving. We haven't reached the Ravendrake caves yet." He continued walking along the base of the mountain.

Laci caught up to Hallvard with questions. "So, what you're saying is that when this dragon gets rid of that rock, it'll turn back into a human?"

Ethan's mouth began to open, so she turned her back to him and avoided his look altogether.

"Exactly. But the rock passes slowly. It could be many moons before she is human again."

Clearly irritated, Thuban increased his pace.

Digger scrambled to climb up the side and entered a small cave.

"Digger is going into a cave. Maybe this is the one!" Penny eagerly said.

"No, it's too small for a mother dragon to birth a young," Hallvard started.

Laci finished. "Not to mention we're still probably in Chuvashian territory, and Digger is a Ravendrake."

Ethan began mumbling, "I'm sick and tired of this journey. I don't know anything about these things, and I don't care. Let's dump this dragon so we can go home, play some

Xbox, and someone can buy me a new phone." He looked at Hallvard. "I think that should be you."

"This cave might be a good place to rest, though," Laci suggested as she ignored Ethan's rant, climbed into it, and sat down. Her bent posture revealed that her stomach pains were back, and her squinted eyes showed her headache was turning into an ocular migraine. That pain typically led to her experiencing *Alice-in-Wonderland* syndrome, which made it impossible to determine distances and sizes. It was obvious that she needed to rest. "Maybe one of my books will have something that helps us determine the right cave for Digger." She unzipped her backpack and pulled out a book.

The others followed her in and sat down while she read.

"What are you doing?" Thuban appeared in the mouth of the cave after doubling back to find them.

"I just thought we could look up Ravendrakes in my *Dragon Field Guide* and—"

"Put that away! I don't need a book to tell me about Ravendrakes!" Thuban snapped. "We don't have time to sit around."

Hallvard reacted to Thuban's orders and Laci's weakness by saying, "No, we rest here."

Laci looked over at him, her shining knight.

Taken aback, Thuban responded to Hallvard, "If we stay to rest, it will be dark before we make it to the Ravendrake birthing caves."

"We need to rest," Hallvard said as he stood and took a step toward Thuban.

"We need to stay alive, you stupid boy."

Hallvard turned around and sat next to Laci.

"Then stay here and die. I'm moving on ahead. You there," Thuban waved his finger toward Buzz, "get that baby up and follow me."

Buzz looked at Ethan and Penny, then to Laci.

"Well, I'm going with him." Ethan got up and stood next to Thuban, who didn't seem to care either way that Ethan had chosen him.

Buzz patted Digger on the head, got his attention, and followed Ethan's lead. Penny looked at her friend, who was clearly suffering, but decided it was best for them to keep moving.

"Come on, Laci, let's go." Penny walked toward Thuban.

"But, Penny, I can't!" Laci cried out, almost in tears.

"We're all tired." Penny wasn't in the mood for guilt. "Laci, I'm constantly coming to your rescue. I know you're weak, but you can't expect all of us to sit here waiting for you to rest and not make it to return this thing before dark." She waved her arm toward Digger and walked to the mouth of the cave.

Laci looked brokenhearted but also angered by Penny's comment that she was weak. "Fine!" She got up and tried to get the backpack on, but the weight of it made her fall over.

"Allow me to help. I will carry that for you," Hallvard offered as he reached down for the pack.

Penny glared at Laci, who was allowing him to take it. She ran over and grabbed the backpack out of Hallvard's hands. "I'll carry it. I have to take care of everything, apparently."

As she stormed off, Laci called to her, "Penny, it's not zipped!"

Penny dropped it onto the ground and zipped it up, but in her haste, she only closed the front zipper; the back one was still halfway open.

CHAPTER EIGHTEEN

THE MOOD OF THE group was decidedly dismal. Not only were they coming away from their first big fight, but they had to drag their feet through thick swampy plants.

Penny, who, due to recent events, disliked vines and almost all vegetation, was glad she'd worn her combat boots as the others struggled to keep their shoes from disappearing in the ankle-deep muck. She replayed the fight with Laci in her head, defending her choice to keep moving. Why should she always concede when it came to Laci's issues? Deep down, she knew it was because Laci was her best friend and that was what friends did. Her train of thought was broken when they departed the swampy muck and reached some short grass. More important, they finally reached the eastern side of the mountain.

The sun was low in the sky, and the mountain blocked what was left of its light, causing that side to be much darker. Their pace looked more like a death march than a group on a mission, but they had to figure out where to leave Digger before dark, when they'd become easy pickings for anything that hunted at night.

"How exactly do we know which house is his?" Buzz asked as he gave a woeful look to Digger.

"Since we are returning him to his birthing chamber, we have to hope he recognizes the smell. Then we will know he is home. If we must return him to his lair, we will have to climb," Hallvard explained.

"I sure hope they don't live in the penthouse. I can't climb that high," Ethan added, looking up at the caves hundreds of yards above them. "And I couldn't call anyone for help if I got stuck up there since my phone is ruined."

"OMG, Ethan. Get over it. It was a piece of junk anyhow, and it wasn't any more useful than a paper cup and a string out here in this place." Penny was sick of him complaining. She was sick of everything at the moment. "My stupid dress will cost more to replace than your cheap old phone."

Hallvard broke the tension. "Well, Ethan, you will not have to climb that high. The upper caves are for the largest of the male dragons. Then the middle level is for the females and their young before they go out on their own, which can take years. So we will concentrate on getting this dragon back to his birthing chamber."

Thuban stared at Ethan. "You wouldn't last the morning trying to climb up the mountain before you became some creature's breakfast." His tone lacked any humor.

Laci added, "The babies don't learn how to fly for a few months, so they need to be able to crawl out to learn to hunt on the ground."

"So they could be in the grass out hunting right now?" Ethan looked out at the grass, but didn't see anything moving. "Fantastic. If they don't eat us on the way there, they can munch on us on the way back."

The pace of the group slowed, so Hallvard used the opportunity to look into some of the lower caves.

Penny slammed the heavy backpack onto the ground. "I hope we need all this stuff because this is ridiculously heavy."

Even Thuban took this opportunity to catch his breath and sat next to Laci, who was wiping muck off her shoes.

Assuming it was a friend plopping down next to her, Laci turned her head and smiled at her visitor, but immediately her disposition changed, causing her to look incredibly uncomfortable.

Penny wasn't exactly sure why Laci didn't like him but suspected it had something to do with him challenging Hallvard as leader of their expedition. She quickly glanced at Hallvard, who vanished out of sight as he continued to climb up to all the lower-level caves. She looked back at Laci, who had been watching Hallvard as well.

Laci snapped her head down and buried her face in her wadded-up hoodie. Penny knew Laci was mad at her for teaming up with Thuban, who was gruff and smelled that funny old-man smell like Roy, instead of Hallvard, who was so chivalrous, knew all about dragons, and smelled great, for a guy who lacked access to indoor plumbing. Penny watched Laci press her head with her hands, a sure sign the pain behind her eyes was increasing and her vision was getting worse and worse. She also knew that the pain in her head was inconsequential compared to the pain of the fight she'd had with her best friend.

Hallvard sprinted back to the group. "Follow me. There is a vacant cave in which it appears the mother gave birth not more than a week ago." This news infused new energy into the group.

Buzz followed with Digger close behind. The others got up one by one. After about thirty yards, they came to a section of rock that presented some challenges.

The entrance to the cave stood at least ten feet off the ground, with a crevice just north of the cave's opening, which they had to climb through. Hallvard traversed the gap with little effort.

"Buzz, pick up Digger and hand him to me." Hallvard lay on his stomach and reached down toward Buzz, who attempted to grab Digger and pick him up.

Digger, however, played a game of *grab and run in circles around Buzz,* which appeared to be much more fun than being picked up.

"Ethan, can you help him?" asked Hallvard.

Ethan had clearly been enjoying the game and had shown no intention of helping, but after Penny's glare reached him, he walked over to corral Digger.

Thuban stood off to the side and kept a watchful eye toward the sky for any unwanted visitors. He didn't aide their attempt to catch the baby dragon.

Digger had apparently found that having two people chase him was even more fun than having one. Ethan eventually stopped in his pursuit, while Buzz kept chasing.

"Why don't we all go up there and have Digger follow us?" Penny suggested.

Laci grabbed her backpack while giving an icy stare to Penny, who had discarded it on the ground again. She then climbed into the crevice while Hallvard extended his hand to help her up. Laci could barely get up the first rock with the heavy backpack.

"Let me hold that for you," offered Thuban.

Penny ran over and took the pack off Laci's back. "I've got it," she said as she strapped it over her own shoulders.

Penny gave Laci a boost without saying anything to her. Hallvard lifted her the rest of the way and practically tossed her now-lightweight frame into the cave.

Ethan kept glancing back to the tall grass, searching for predators, stepping in front of Penny, then making the climb.

Penny went next. She was almost at the top when she slipped, mostly due to the extra weight throwing off her balance. She slammed her side into one of the rocks to keep from falling all the way back down, but the jolt smacked the backpack, and several books fell out, including the journal. The books landed on some rocks below, teetering on the edge of the deep crevice, which disappeared under the mountain. She reached for them, but they were just out of range.

Thuban saw the books and also reached to grab them, but, as he did, they disappeared down the crevice. Penny's heart sank; she dove down onto the rocks and shoved her hand in, scraping her arm and cheek.

"Be careful. You should not reach your hand as such. A myriad of creatures could reside there," Hallvard warned.

Penny didn't care. Without the journal, they were stuck. Her heart raced as she felt things crawling on her arm, causing her imagination to run wild. In a brief state of panic, she yanked her arm out and expeditiously smashed every creature attached to her skin. Never a quitter, she took a deep breath, plunged her hand back in, and felt around for the books. Instantly, the arthropods resumed gnawing at her flesh. "Really?" she asked them as she continued to search.

The textbooks were bigger and easier to identify and push aside, but she was having trouble locating the journal. *I can't give up now. Everyone is counting on me.* Just as she thought this, some thing or things agonizingly bit her. She could feel the blood trickle down her arm to her palm, making her hand slippery. *Concentrate and find that journal.* She felt it, not the whole thing, just a corner; she couldn't get a good grip. The throbbing bites took a toll, making it difficult to focus. Sweat poured down her face and stung her eyes.

She reached out again, and as pain shot up from her hand, she realized her arm was stretching, not merely attaining a better position, but actually growing, just enough to get a good grip on the journal. She squeezed it with her fingers and pulled it out of the crevice, then swatted at the multitude of insects feasting on her arm. Small blood trails trickled down her elbow, which she wiped off with the bottom of her dress. Releasing a deep breath, she put the journal back into the backpack and zipped it up all the way. "Pain is a symptom of the effort," she said to herself, quoting the meme on the inside of her locker. On the athletic field, the ability to overcome pain had served her well, as was the case today. The scare of almost losing the journal gave her an adrenaline boost, and she easily climbed to the mouth of the cave.

Buzz attempted to climb, but climbing wasn't his forte. He held on to the side while his feet pedaled the air ineffectively. Thuban shook his head and reluctantly gave him a boost. Hallvard pulled him the rest of the way. When Buzz got to the top, he looked below to find Digger but couldn't see him anywhere. "Oh no, he's gone." Buzz had barely finished his sentence when he turned around and saw the baby dragon behind him, ready for another game of chase. "There you are. Good boy!" Buzz grinned as he pet Digger's head but then immediately pulled jarfalla leaves out of his pocket and started to wipe his hands clean.

Hallvard called down to Thuban, "Are you coming up?"

Thuban replied, "I had better stay down here and keep watch."

They stood at the edge of the cave. "You already checked it out, and there's no dragon inside?" asked a cautious Laci.

"No women eating rocks?" Buzz asked.

"Yes, I checked it out," Hallvard reassured them.

Ethan picked up a strange object he found on the ground and flipped it back and forth, trying to figure out what it was. "How do you know that this is Digger's home?"

"Well, I won't be sure until he goes in and recognizes it, but that pile of afterbirth you're playing with tells me that a baby was birthed here recently," Hallvard said.

Ethan threw down the blob of dried innards and wiped his hands on his pants and then on Buzz's shirt.

The cave was extremely large and went deep into the mountain. Their footsteps echoed as they moved closer to the back. The farther they went, the more intense the smell of methane. "Wow, this cave is big," Buzz said as he pushed Digger with his hands, covered once again in jarfalla leaves. He'd stuffed a lot of them up his sleeves and in his pockets; in fact, he'd even stuffed some down his shirt, making him look a bit pudgy.

All of a sudden, Digger stopped as he sniffed the air. He shook his head back and forth and let out a loud screech. Everyone in the cave covered their ears.

Digger hopped up and down and let out another ear-shattering screech. "I guess this must be the right cave," said Penny. "Shall we go now?"

"Yes," says Hallvard. "We need to get out of here." They ran to the front of the cave, with Digger chasing them and shrieking all the way.

As they approached the opening, they heard Thuban yell, "Hurry, get out of there."

It was too late. Out of the fog came a giant female Ravendrake dragon. She was the same dragon that chased them when they'd first arrived in that realm. Their escape route was cut off as mama landed on the edge of the entrance. She spread her wings, blocking the entire cave opening, then let out a cry so loud it knocked them off their feet.

Digger replied to her cry with one of his own. The sound inside the cave was so loud they could feel it in their bones. Laci's pained expression made it obvious she felt it in her head.

They backed up, tripping over each other until they were pressed against the rear wall of the cave. "When I attack the dragon, make your escape," a rather uneasy Hallvard said as he pulled out the dagger that had killed the stygg.

"With that? You're out of your mind," said Penny.

The mother dragon slowly walked toward them. She rolled her head in a forward circle, slashing at the air with her horns.

"We brought your baby back. We didn't mean to take him. Please don't kill us!" Buzz yelled hysterically.

The dragon responded with another blood-curdling scream and continued to approach them.

Just when they thought it was over, and Buzz was stumbling over poorly worded Hail Marys, an arm protruded out of a small crevice and grabbed Penny, who screamed. Her scream triggered the rest of them to scream, which temporarily mesmerized the dragon. A man moved the rocks behind them aside and, still gripping her arm, managed to squeeze Penny through the small opening in the back of the cave. The backpack got caught, but Penny jerked it through. He grabbed Laci next, and Ethan eagerly followed. Hallvard was poised with his dagger, waiting for Buzz to follow the others, but Buzz didn't budge.

"Buzz! Follow them," Hallvard shouted.

Buzz stood paralyzed.

"Buzz! Buzz! There are fresh baked rolls behind you through that opening."

"What?" Buzz squeezed through, and Hallvard slipped in behind him.

The man pulled Hallvard toward him and yelled, "Down!"

All of them dove to the cave floor as a stream of fire shot through the small gap they had just entered. The fire illuminated the tunnel, which seemed to continue endlessly in both directions.

"Everybody up. Run!" They jumped to their feet as he led them down an inner tunnel. The tunnel quickly narrowed, causing them to hunch over and look more at their feet than where they were headed. Not that being upright would have aided their visuals. It was pitch-black, with the only light coming from a torch the old man held out in front of him, and that light was absorbed by the darkness, leaving little to no light at the back of the line.

"I can't see!" Buzz shouted into the black abyss in front of him.

The torch exploded as it passed through a patch of methane gas, causing a chorus of shrieks.

"Okay, that helped, but can you warn me before you do that again, please?" Buzz called out.

The man leading them was not fazed by the repeated burst of flames as he kept a keen and steady pace. Behind him, the group bounced off each other, their shrieks abated as they grew accustomed to the methane patches. They bumped and scraped the tunnel walls and tripped over each other and their own feet.

Laci became dizzy from the gases and the exertion of running. She caught her foot on the back of Penny's and fell into her, causing Penny to slam into the cave wall. As she pulled away, they heard a ripping noise.

"Great! Now you've torn my dress for the wedding. Thanks a lot." She helped Laci to her feet and pulled her along behind her, careful of Laci's unsteady gait. As angry as she was, she wouldn't leave Laci behind in this maze of certain death.

Ahead of them, the man made a quick left without breaking stride. The group managed to follow only because another burst of fire shot from his torch just before he turned, illuminating the fork. This new tunnel seemed as endless as the last. The old man kept his steady pace, although at a diminished speed, for which the group was grateful. After a few minutes, he slowed to a walk and turned to his right.

Penny could see light in the distance, not bright sunlight, since it was setting, but they were finally free of the engulfing utter darkness. The tunnel had opened into a cave on the south side of the mountain. Each stopped to catch a breath as they entered the cave.

"You can't rest. We need to move down through the small valley and up that hillside across from us," the man said as he pointed out toward the distance.

"We've been running for like twenty minutes. I need a break," Laci said, doubled over and gasping for air.

"What about the old guy?" asked Buzz between gasps for air. "Don't we need to get him?"

The stranger looked intently at Buzz. "You can't go back that way, and it's suicide to travel around at night. Your friend will have to make it on his own."

"He'll be okay," Hallvard quickly answered. "There's nothing we can do for him now," he said as he reluctantly glanced over at the man who had just rescued them, nodding and bowing to him. "I am Hallvard of Botkyrka. Who must I thank for saving my friends and myself?"

The older man was somewhere in the neighborhood of sixty years old but in great shape, with tan, leathery skin, and large, strong hands. He didn't have time to respond before Penny spoke.

"We should help him. Thuban is the one who got us here. Without him, we'd all be dead, including you."

"Penny's right," Ethan added.

Laci lashed out at Ethan, "Of course you think Penny's right."

"Me? You blindly follow this guy, no matter what he says." He pointed to Hallvard.

Hallvard put his hand on Ethan's shoulder to try and calm him down as the older man stepped back and watched their behavior intently, studying them and their clothes. Ethan pulled his shoulder away.

"You just have a crush on him and aren't thinking straight," Penny yelled to Laci as she pointed at Hallvard.

"Thuban is the one who really got us here to return Buzz's love child."

"We never would have met Thuban if Hallvard hadn't saved us from Digger's angry mother!" Laci shouted back.

"Saved us? He nearly drowned us!" Penny responded.

"Well, you almost lost the journal, which is our only hope to get home, by leaving my backpack unzipped, even though I told you to zip it when you ripped it away from us."

"Us? What, are you married now? And I didn't almost lose it. It just fell down onto the rock. I totally saw it," Penny snapped back.

"ENOUGH!" Buzz yelled. "I can't take it. First I have to give my new best friend away, and you two, the biggest BFFs ever, are screaming at each other. I can't take it!" Buzz followed his outburst with a dramatic silence that got everyone's attention.

Hesitantly, Hallvard asked, "Are we done?" When nobody responded, he looked at the older man and repeated his question.

CHAPTER NINETEEN

"WHO I AM IS irrelevant. Who are you, and what on earth were you doing in a birthing cave? Are you insane?" The man lectured them on their stupidity. "I could tell you weren't pirates. Just look at you. Did you think this would be a fun little adventure? Go see the dragons where they live?"

The group was too embarrassed to speak.

"Were you even aware that you were being followed by a couple of pirates?"

Buzz spun around as if they were right behind him.

"Thuban said that would happen," Penny defended the absent member of their party.

All of the kids looked at the ground as if there would be some magical answer there to tell them what to do next.

The mysterious man continued his rant. "It's late, and it's not safe to stay here. Between the pirates, the Vardo, and Glem fog you won't last two hours. I live over there on top of that hill. You can sleep there tonight." He pointed to a hilltop, which appeared to be empty. He was met with a sea of confused looks.

"We appreciate your kindness." Hallvard expressed his gratitude.

Not to ever let anything go, Buzz chimed in. "Who is Glem Fog?"

The weathered man turned to respond to Buzz's very naïve question. "It's not a who. It's a what. Glem fog is a combination of the dragon's breath and the unnatural atmosphere surrounding the mountain. If you breathe too much of it, you'll become disoriented and probably wander around in circles until something eats you. It's strongest at night."

Buzz looked terrified. "I don't want that."

"I don't want that either. Everyone needs to stick close to me," the older man instructed.

Laci retrieved her battered backpack and made sure every zipper was secure. As she lifted it, she felt Hallvard assist her and place it on her back. Although she wouldn't get over losing her perfect standing at the library, deep down Laci was grateful for the diminished load that occupied the pack.

"Follow me and stay as low to the ground as you can. We'll travel along the tree line until it ends. The dragons hunt at dusk, so this is their prime feeding time, but there's nothing we can do about that now." The older man pointed at Hallvard. "You make sure nobody falls behind."

Hallvard nodded.

The man headed down a small path that led to some tall grass on the edge of the tree line. They moved through the trees quickly. He showed no hesitation as he maneuvered across the uneven ground. The group struggled to keep up with him. This was no place to be when the sun went down.

Penny kept up alongside him, explaining her group's actions. "For your information, we were returning a baby dragon to its mother to save a village from being destroyed."

The hardened man looked at her straight in the eyes with a cold un-telling stare and came to an abrupt stop.

"I accept your apology—" Penny said as he grabbed her by the arm and yanked her to the top of the steep embankment.

"Stay here," he told her.

Laci watched and waited for a response from Penny, who never liked being told what to do, especially by strangers, but being as far out of her element as she had ever been, she surprisingly obeyed.

One by one, he headed back down the embankment to assist each of them up, with Hallvard pushing from below. Ethan resisted help from either and fell flat on his butt in some mossy soil when he lost his grip. He scrambled and stubbornly made it up to join the others. As they stood at the top of the embankment, only an open meadow with some tall grass lay between them and the top of the knoll where he claimed his home was, although at this point they'd yet to see it.

"What about the snakes and booby traps?" Buzz referred to the castle they had seen the day before as he looked around.

The old man ignored his question.

Because they'd come out on the south side, they were currently traveling in the land of the Hellblaze Wyverns, definitely not a breed to be taken lightly.

"When I give the signal, move, and don't stop until you reach the top of the hill and safety," he told them.

"What's the signal?" Buzz asked.

"Run!" shouted the man.

Without hesitation, and following his advice, they kept to his heels. Without Digger dragging him down, Buzz was much faster now, leaving Laci and her burdensome backpack trailing behind all alone. Hallvard, with his chivalrous nature, swooped her up under his arm like the Sunday paper, and caught up to the others.

Their movement attracted the attention of a few flame-breathing giants, who lifted off from the perches of their various caves and headed straight for the group. Their blood-red chests had rolls of armor, giving the appearance of six-pack abs. Two horns jutted back away from their faces on either side of their head, like angry Spock ears. Their talons were by far bigger and sharper than any other dragon they'd seen on this charming vacation. Their wings displayed a ragged appearance at the bottom, but there wasn't enough time to study them to see if they'd come that way, or if they'd been torn in battle.

"Above!" Hallvard yelled and pointed back toward the mountain.

Shooting flames and screeching at a pitch higher than should be possible, the Hellblaze Wyverns came in for the kill. With talons outstretched at the end of its muscular legs, one of them aimed for Hallvard and Laci. The pressure of the down draft from its massive wings bore upon them.

Hallvard pulled Laci to his chest and lunged into the tall grass, rolling away from the beast. The Wyvern dove and grabbed at them but was unable to secure a grip. One talon, however, made contact with Laci's leg, ripping a gash into her thigh, twelve inches long and half-an-inch wide. It felt like her leg had caught fire, and she screamed accordingly. Hallvard threw his jerkin over them in an attempt to make them look like a mound of dirt in the tall grass.

The other Wyvern shrieked a victory cry as it impaled its prey and lifted it off the ground.

Penny, who labored to keep up with their guide, stopped and looked in horror, trying to identify who had become the Wyvern's victim. In the darkness, she couldn't make out the figure as it sailed away in the sky and landed on the other side of the hilltop. She turned around to count her friends, but the man yanked her arm again, jerking her head forward.

The Wyvern let out another shriek as it ripped apart its victim.

"No!" Penny screamed as he yanked her over the top of the grassy knoll, opened a door built into the hillside, and dragged her in.

Meanwhile, Hallvard and Laci were still pinned down in the grass by the other Wyvern who kept circling, searching for the animal it had wounded.

"Lie still," Hallvard told Laci. He rolled over on his back while keeping his jerkin over the top of the two of them.

The Wyvern heard the calls of its mate and lifted off the ground to join in the kill.

"Can you stand and run?" he asked her.

"I think so. It just hurts so much."

He put his arm around her and gave her a hug. "Laci, you have come this far. I have seen your bravery. I know you can do this. I will not leave you. When I say go, we run all the way to the top of the hill," he said with confidence.

He helped her to her knees, keeping his arm around her. Then he scanned the sky for more dragons, but none were in sight. "Run, now!" he said, and they headed up the hill. Hallvard held her side as she limped up the final embankment but collapsed before they reached the top.

Inside the modest cabin, it was dusty and sparse but felt solid and secure. Penny and the man had to walk down a set of stairs to enter because the structure was predominantly underground. The windows had sturdy wooden shutters, which he opened on all sides of the studio-style abode, giving him a three-hundred-and-sixty-degree view of his surroundings. A small bed filled the corner facing the mountain, and across from that was a desk and chair with stacks of books and papers everywhere. To the left of the desk was a tiny kitchen-like area with some apples and carrots stacked in wooden bowls along with some kind of salted jerky that hung from a hook in the low ceiling.

Ethan burst through the door and collapsed onto the dirt floor.

"Ethan, where's Buzz?" Penny asked.

Ethan took a quick look around the cottage and didn't see him. "He was in front of me. I thought he was already here."

Penny started pacing back and forth. "They should all be here by now. I never should have left Laci."

Just then, the door opened and Hallvard entered carrying a bleeding Laci.

"Oh, thank God you are alive." She ran over and hugged Laci, who was still in his arms. "You're bleeding!"

"She was almost caught by that Wyvern." Hallvard set her down on the bed and started tending to the wound. "Sir, do you have any mjodurt clusters? I need to make a dressing to stave off infection."

Although she was in extreme pain, glancing over at her handsome caretaker seemed to ease some of it. Doc Sheinblatt back home couldn't hold a candle to Hallvard.

"We have to find Buzz," said Ethan, as he headed for the door.

"I think the dragon got him," said Penny. She grabbed Ethan's arm to stop him, and tears welled in her eyes.

"What?" Ethan shouted.

"I saw the one dragon fly off with him in his grip," Penny explained.

"Are you sure it was Buzz?" asked Ethan, who began to tear up as well.

Everyone was looking at Penny in anticipation. "Well, I don't know. It was hard to tell, but he's the only one not here."

Before she could finish her sentence, the door opened. "Man, why don't you have a doorbell or something? I've been crawling around out there trying to find the stupid door." Buzz entered out of breath, but like always, still able to talk.

Ethan and Penny ran over and hugged him. Buzz appeared shocked at their affection but also seemed to enjoy it.

After a prolonged hug, Penny finally released Buzz and asked, "But if the dragon didn't get one of us, what did it pick up?"

The hardened man pointed through one of the windows. "See for yourself." Penny and Ethan stood on their tiptoes to look out and saw the two Wyverns ripping apart creatures that looked like a cross between a sheep and a wolf.

Buzz was still a little too short to see out of the high and narrow windows, so he jumped up and down to try to get a glimpse. "I wanna see. What is it?"

"It's called an Ulvsau. I let two of them out into the pasture when I suspected I was going to need a distraction getting home." The old man turned away and headed toward the kitchen area.

"Why did you build your house here? I mean, don't you think it's kind of dangerous?" Buzz asked as he followed him toward the food area. The man stopped for a second but didn't turn around to answer.

While Penny and the others gazed out the window to watch the Wyverns at work, Laci looked around for something to keep the blood from dripping on the bed. She opened her backpack with one hand and pilfered through the books. Unfortunately, her textbooks had that plastic coating on the paper, so those pages weren't absorbent. The journal had a thick soft paper, but she certainly didn't want to tear any possible instructions out. She flipped to the back and found several blank pages. Tearing out a sheet, she winced as she pressed it against her gaping wound.

Within seconds, the bleeding and the pain stopped. Laci looked down in astonishment and saw that the wound had closed up. She gazed at the journal page. *How can this be?* she thought. Flipping through the journal and studying the pages with objects correlating to the ones in the box made her wonder what else this book was capable of. It had clearly opened portals to other worlds and had healing powers. As she marveled over this, she suddenly cringed as she wondered what harm could be done if the book fell into the wrong hands. She decided to keep her new discovery and thoughts to herself and covered her leg with a blanket.

The Wyverns finished one Ulvsau and took the remains of the other back to the mountain. Seizing the opportunity, the man went out the back door.

"For such a small cabin, two doors seems a bit excessive," Penny said as she looked around. "But I suppose I won't mention it to him since he probably just gave up his meat supply for the next two months to save our butts."

He returned with what looked like cotton balls.

"What's that?" Buzz asked.

"Mjodurt flowers are used on cuts to kill infections and quicken healing," Hallvard explained as he reached for them.

"It smells like beer!" Ethan turned his nose up.

"They are also used to make mjod, a type of ale," Laci added.

"What are you doing here and why?" This time the man seemed to demand the information.

The room went silent. Hallvard leaned over Laci, who quickly crumpled up the journal page and stuffed it into her hoodie pocket. He subtly shook his head no, signaling for her not to say anything about the journal or their situation.

"I told you, we were returning the baby to stop the mother from destroying the village," Penny repeated.

Obviously unsatisfied with the answer, the man stood at the window and stared out at the mountain without another word. An uncomfortable quiet filled the tiny room. Not even Buzz seemed to want to break the silence. Hallvard looked at the gash in Laci's thigh, but as he wiped the smeared blood away, he noticed the wound had substantially healed. He put the mjodurt clusters on her leg.

She gazed at him, smiling.

"Does that not sting?" he asked.

"Um, I guess a little." Laci wasn't sure what to say. It didn't hurt at all, and pain tolerance wasn't one of her specialties. She pushed the page deeper into her hoodie pocket to conceal it, knowing that they were obviously powerful, whether or not the pages had writing.

"You have magic in you, don't you, Miss Laci?" Hallvard smiled and picked up the rest of the mjodurt clusters. "I guess you don't need any more of this."

That got the attention of the man, who pivoted away from the window and stared at Laci.

She stared back, trying not to give anything away.

He turned back to the window and continued his lookout.

Laci had never stared anyone down. She wondered if maybe the adventure was giving her a newfound confidence. Then she wondered if she would live through it or even make it home to show off her new confidence.

"Miss Penny, may I see your leg where the vine cut your skin?" Hallvard asked.

She sat on the desk chair and pulled her skirt up over her knee.

"This may sting, or not."

Ethan kept a close eye on Hallvard as he pressed the clusters against her wound.

"OUCH!" she cried out. "That's like lime juice on a paper cut!" Her outburst got a chuckle from the man who didn't bother to turn around. Penny, however, turned bright red. "Stupid stinging beer flowers."

"It will hurt for a bit but shall keep you from infection." Hallvard looked into her eyes and smiled. It was almost a sad smile; then he gave her a hug, which caused Laci to sit up a little straighter in bed. "You need to take your shoes off for the medicine to flow unrestricted..." He helped her take them off and caught a glimpse of the jewel as she tried to stuff it into the toe of her boot without anyone seeing. "...just while you sleep. When morning comes, it will be fine to put them back on."

Buzz looked over. "What's going to happen in the morning?"

Hallvard exchanged a glance with the man and replied, "We shall discuss it then. It's late now, so why don't we all get some rest." The man handed out a few blankets before he closed and locked all the shutters, making the room almost completely dark.

Curled up on the floor with their rolled-up blankets under their heads, Buzz and Ethan fell asleep immediately.

Laci moved over to make room for Penny to join her on the bed. Instinctively, Penny hugged Laci and whispered into her ear, "I'm sorry I yelled at you. I'm so glad you're okay, I don't know what I'd do without you."

Laci hugged Penny back even harder as a few tears of relief rolled down her face. The two let go of each other, and Laci squeezed her backpack. Penny wedged her boots between the bed and the wall. Both of them fell fast asleep the moment their heads hit the pillow.

Laci was soon deep asleep, and her mind relived the Wyvern attack. But in this perception, she witnessed the events from the viewpoint of the dragon. The light was dim, but her vision was perfectly clear. She could see each detail, every blade of grass. She watched Penny and the others scramble up the hill, and instinctively she dove down, going in for the kill. As she got closer, she realized the person she was about to kill was Hallvard. This realization jerked her out of her dream, but seconds later, she was fast asleep again.

Morning came all too soon; the nights were short this time of year. Sunrise flooded the room as the man began opening the shutters. Penny and Laci smiled at seeing each other, and a quick hug reiterated that all was forgiven.

"Your friend is gone," the man said matter-of-factly.

They looked around the room spotting Buzz and Ethan still sleeping on the floor, but no Hallvard.

"He must be out gathering food or something." Laci defended him. "He would never just leave us."

Penny jumped up and grabbed her boots. Fishing in one toe, then the other, she found nothing. "It's gone," she whispered to Laci. "The jewel is gone."

A sickening feeling hit Laci in the pit of her stomach, and it wasn't the lack of food or the grey gruel anymore. She knew what she was going to find, but she had to check anyway. Reluctantly, she reached for her backpack and slowly unzipped it. The journal had to be there. Hallvard was a hero; he would never hurt or abandon her. He'd just saved her life. As she dug through every pocket, her heart broke. The journal was gone.

She tried to convince herself that someone else must have done it. What about the strange man? It could have been him, but then her fingers stumbled across some paper. It was another page torn from the journal. On it was written:

My dearest Laci,

It pains me to take this from you without explanation. Know in your heart that I will return to get you safely home, once I have done what I need to do.

Stay at the cabin where you are safe, and I promise my help for you and your friends.

Yours most sincerely,
Hallvard

Laci burst into tears. Her entire world had been shattered with one letter.

CHAPTER TWENTY

LACI SAT ON THE bed sobbing. Penny was too upset to console her friend.

"What's wrong?" The man glared at Penny, whom he'd clearly established as the leader of the group.

"It's nothing." Penny was too distraught to come up with a good excuse to appease him.

Ethan and Buzz woke up, rubbing their eyes and yawning.

"What's wrong with Laci?" Ethan asked. No one answered him.

Buzz wandered into the kitchen-area and poked around at the food.

"Answer me," the man insisted. "What's going on? I can't help you if you don't tell me what the problem is."

Penny was taken aback. That was the first time the man had asked, instead of dictated. Penny wondered if he actually intended to help them or if he, too, had planned to double-cross them.

"Hey, where's Hallvard?" Buzz asked as he bounced an apple in his hand, looking oblivious to everything going on around him. "Is that why Laci is crying? I'm sure he'll be right back. Maybe he's out getting more of that mojurt stuff. Oh, maybe he's picking berries. I love berries. They're great mixed with pineapple. Oh, pineapple... I wonder if he can find some pineapple."

"He isn't outside. He left," explained Penny.

"Oh well, now that we returned the dragon, I guess we don't need him anymore," Ethan said.

"Yeah, but he took the journal with him when he left," Penny said quietly.

"Are you kidding me? We can't get home without the journal," Ethan said.

"No, he didn't," Buzz mumbled with a mouthful of apple.

Penny turned around to see Buzz at the desk.

"What did you say, Buzz?" Laci asked.

Clearing his mouth of food, he answered, "I said no, he didn't. It's right here." He held up a book that looked remarkably similar.

"That's mine," The excitement was short-lived as the man snatched the book from Buzz and locked it into his desk.

"Hey, that's ours," accused Penny.

"No, that's not it. The cover of ours is different, older, and more worn," said Laci.

"Where did you get that journal?" The man's attitude returned to his grumpy old self.

"You wouldn't know the place, but we need it to find our way home," said Penny.

"Did you use the journal to get here?" the man questioned. The room went silent.

The two boys stared at Penny and Laci.

"I'll take that as a yes," said the man, who immediately grabbed his coat and satchel and proceeded to fill it with apples, bread, and jerky. "We need to stop him, and if you kids ever want to get back to your home, you need to tell me the exact location where you arrived." The silence continued. "Now!" he yelled at them.

They all shrank a little. He was grumpy before, but that seemed to have escalated to anger.

Laci began crying again.

The old man softened. "We have to cut your friend off. If he leaves with the journal, you're stuck here. Please, where did you enter this land?"

Penny was confused. She wondered how the guy knew they'd traveled here from another land, other than by her hideous dress.

"We landed on that grassy hill," Buzz said.

"I'm going to need a little more information than that."

Although Hallvard introduced himself with it all the time, Penny couldn't remember the village name. "His village."

"Botkyrka," Laci remembered, of course.

"Ah, the grassy knoll by the woodshed," he mumbled to himself.

"Yeah, that's what I said," Buzz took credit.

Energy filled the room with the realization that the man could be their ticket home.

"And where's the key?" he asked.

They all looked toward Laci. "But we never found a key. It wasn't locked."

"The artifact," the man explained. "When placed on the page, it opens the portal."

"The emerald," Laci said.

With everyone optimistically looking at her, Penny shook her head. "Hallvard stole that, too."

"Okay, no time to waste. Get up and let's go." He unlocked the desk, grabbed his journal, and stuck it into his jacket, as well as a few more apples and jerky.

"What about breakfast?" Buzz asked.

"I'm starving, too," Ethan added. The man tossed them all apples.

"This will have to do for now. We don't have much time." The sense of urgency in his voice was nerve-wracking.

"How will he know how to use it?" asked Laci as she zipped her backpack and mounted it on her shoulders.

The man stopped, stared her in the eyes, and with a chilling seriousness in his voice, responded, "You have no idea what you've done. We can't rely on the assumption that he won't be able to open the portal. We have to stop him."

"Hey, it's not her fault." Penny defended Laci.

The man froze for a moment, his mouth opened as if to speak, then closed, and he headed for the door. The girls and Buzz followed him. Ethan, however, didn't move.

"You'll do exactly what I say and not ask questions..." The man stated and looked sternly from Ethan to Buzz. "...if you want to make it out alive."

After ushering them out, he pulled the door to lock it and noticed Ethan still planted in the middle of the room. "I realize this is a lot to ask of you, but we have no other choice. And we might get lucky. If the pirates get him, we could stumble across his corpse with the journal in his pocket. Of course, the jewel will be gone. If the dragons or the Vardos get him, we're in big trouble. So, let's hope it's the pirates."

"Okay, let's go," Penny yelled impatiently, coaxing Ethan to reluctantly head out the door. She regretted yelling immediately. He was done with this trip, and she didn't blame him in the least.

The skies were free of dragons as they walked down to the tree line. "Daybreak is the best time to travel. The dragons aren't early risers," the man said.

Arriving at the end of the tree line, he picked up a few sticks and pulled out a bunch of tall, dry grass. Wrapping the grass around one end and tying them with more grass, he fashioned a few torches. He handed one to Penny and kept the others, then signaled everyone to run. They raced across the last area of unprotected space and entered the mouth of the cave opening that led to the tunnel. Once in the safety of the vacant cave, he gave them one last piece of advice. "Please keep your eyes open for the Vardos. We're going through early enough that they should still be sleeping, as are most of the dragons. However, the Vardos are light sleepers and, if you wake them, they punish you by cutting your head off. Their method of stunning their opponent is different from the dragons," the man explained. "Don't believe what you see."

When they entered the tunnel opening, the familiar methane smell instantly overwhelmed them, making their stomachs turn.

"Good thing we only had apples for breakfast. I'd hate to have to throw up a full meal," Penny said as she tried to wave the fumes away from her face.

Buzz looked at the fork. Last night had been so chaotic he couldn't remember which tunnel they had come from. "Which way do we go?" he asked, poking his head into one tunnel and then the other.

"We need to exit on the west side, so we'll take this one." The old man pointed to the path on the left, and then he squatted. He lit the torches with a flint he had in his pocket. Handing one back to Penny, he kept the other one for himself and motioned for them to follow.

The tunnel was extremely claustrophobic, and they discovered another new smell they probably could have lived their lives without breathing, sort of an ammonia and straw-steaming brew.

"I'm picturing the witches huddled around a big, black pot with their pointed hats and their green, warty noses, cackling as they stir the latest batch, throwing in a few extra toads and eyes of newt," Ethan joked.

Penny was glad to see his mood had lightened, but the jagged edges of the tunnel walls that surrounded them made her heart beat so fast, she could feel the pounding in her ears. This overwhelming fear wasn't something she was accustomed to. As tough as she was, everyone had a breaking point, and Penny felt she was nearing hers.

Laci's backpack kept snagging on the rough surfaces, and although having slept on a bed helped a little, it was obvious her depth perception wasn't back to normal. She waved her hands wildly in front of her to avoid running into anything.

Buzz began to hyperventilate. "Hey, guys, I don't know if you know this, but a few years ago, me and my brothers and sisters were playing a game of hide and seek. Kevin put me into the dryer and shut it. It seemed like the perfect hiding place, but it wasn't. I freaked out, and I think I'm gonna do it again." Buzz gasped for air.

Laci turned around, accidentally smacking him in the face with her waving arms, and whispered to him, "Are you going to be okay?"

He shook his head no, so she started to gently pat his back to calm him down.

The man shushed them and motioned to keep moving. The hunched-over travel continued for approximately half a mile until the tunnel broadened. Four hundred yards later, they reached an area where they could stand fully upright.

The ceiling rose until it was well above their heads. Buzz rushed out and took a deep breath. "Freedom!"

Away from the two torch carriers, it was too dark to clearly see, and he ran straight into what looked like a pointy sandbag hanging from the ceiling.

As Penny and the man cautiously entered the opening, their torch-light revealed that it wasn't a sandbag at all. Hanging from clawed toes that hooked onto jagged rocks above, it looked like a bat with its arms wrapping a cape around itself. The body twisted toward Buzz, and the sallow-looking female's yellow eyes had sprung open.

"I'm sorry!" Buzz blurted out. "I didn't mean to bump into you. Go back to sleep."

The Vardo flipped herself upright and faced him.

"Wow, that was cool!" Buzz said, regarding her athletic ability.

In response to the commotion, the other Vardos flipped themselves down with ninja-like precision.

As each came down, they squared off with one of the group. It was almost completely dark in there, except for the lights from the two torches. When the Vardos' eyes glowed red, they drew their prey in. Instantly, the Vardo read their mind and transformed into someone their victim found pleasing or soothing, thus taking the fight out of them immediately and making it easier to remove their head.

Since Buzz's witch flipped first, she stared into his eyes and quickly transformed into the form of his mother. Buzz looked mesmerized, comforted and confused all at the same time. As the other Vardos squared off with an individual, they all began to morph.

The one in front of Penny transformed into Zak Effron. She was completely frozen in his presence.

Laci's witch morphed into Hallvard.

Ethan's turned into Anna Sophia Robb, and the old man stood in front of a striking young woman, somewhere in her late teens, wearing a poodle skirt, black and white saddle shoes, and a pink sweater, with her hair in a high ponytail. Penny caught a glimpse of the young woman only briefly but was shaken out of her trance when she saw Anna Sophia Robb with her boney, clawed fingers around Ethan's neck.

She screamed, "No!" Her friends startled, then she promptly landed a right cross to Zak Effron's face. The witch screamed in anger, which reverberated through the cave, knocking everyone back to their senses. The old man pressed his torch against her cape and lit the witch in front of him on fire, which caused all the Vardos to scream. He yelled above the noise. "Come on, this way!"

Buzz and Laci out-maneuvered their witches by smacking them with Laci's backpack. Buzz called back over his shoulder, "Sorry, mom!" as his witch clutched at her battered face.

Penny ran the opposite way to help Ethan, who was pinned against the wall by his witch. He struggled with her, punching and kicking, but she wouldn't let go. Her claws scratched his arms and dug into the skin, leaving trails of blood as her grip tightened. Penny raced up from behind and set the witch's cloak on fire. The Vardo howled in pain and released him.

Their screams were disorienting and caused confusion as to where the exit was.

"This way. Hurry!" the old man yelled as he moved through the westernmost tunnel out of the sleeping chamber.

Laci and Buzz passed him, rushing through the dark.

Penny was still waving her dying torch at the witches, giving her friends a head start before she caught up with them. As she reached the tunnel the man had exited through, she threw the remains of her torch at a group of witches, catching several of them on fire. They shrieked so loud Penny fell to the ground with her palms pressed into her ears to stop the pain.

Ethan tugged on the tattered sleeve of her dress and pulled her off the ground and through the tunnel. They ran like mad.

"I hope there aren't any forks in this tunnel," Penny said as she kept up with Ethan, praying they'd soon find their friends.

When they reached the end of the tunnel and were out into the daylight, they found the old man lighting some dry grass on fire while Buzz and Laci collected more to pile in front of the entrance.

While pulling grass, Buzz said, "That was a close one. I can't believe my mom tried to kill me. Well, sort of."

Ethan shook his head. "You do realize that wasn't your mom."

"Yeah, I know. I miss her even more now," Buzz whispered to himself.

"Speaking of that," Penny said, "Anna Sophia Robb?" She eyed Ethan suspiciously.

"What? I can't help it. I like blondes," Ethan admitted, causing Penny to smirk. "What about yours? Zak Effron? You should be ashamed. How old is he?"

Nobody mentioned the vision of Hallvard that had stood in front of Laci.

Ethan's arm was bleeding badly. He'd held it out of sight, but Laci had bumped into him as she pulled more dry grass, and her leg had been splattered with some blood dripping off his hand. She pulled the journal page out of her hoodie pocket and grabbed his arm. At first, he flinched away.

"Can I just try something? It might help," she sweetly said.

"Fine." Ethan stuck his arm out.

She pressed the paper against the cut, and it immediately stopped the bleeding and began to heal the wound. The pain disappeared as well.

"Monumental," he quietly said her. "Okay, Laci, I admit it. You do know some pretty cool stuff."

She put the blood-soaked paper back into her pocket and returned to stoking the fire. They could hear the witches screech behind the flames.

The man's weathered face looked to the rising sun. "We don't have much time to get another jewel. We'll have to climb. You, and you." He pointed to Buzz and Laci. "Stay here and keep that fire burning. The rest of us will climb and get the jewel."

They began their ascent up the mountain, knowing it would take a while before they reached any caves that might have jewels inside. With daybreak upon them, some of the dragons would head out for their morning hunt soon. They quickly and painstakingly pulled themselves up the rock wall until they found a cave that appeared to be vacant. It was the Taj Mahal of dragon caves.

"This one is vacant, but it's of no use to us," the old man commented and kept climbing the wall.

"Why?" Penny asked.

The old man stopped to get a better grip with his hands as he explained, "There were evil twin dragons that lived here years ago. No other dragon dares to enter, in case they return, and they will someday return."

"I thought only one two-headed evil dragon existed." Penny recalled a story from Hallvard.

"That's from legend. But I lived it. I know there are two."

"How do you know they'll return?" Penny asked.

"Because they haven't been killed. They've only been separated. There's not a man or dragon who can defeat them," he said. He resumed his climb.

"Where are you going?" Ethan called to him. "Can't we take as many of their jewels that we want, then?"

The old man kept climbing as he explained, "They were so evil that their skin would freeze if they slept on these jewels. All the jewels the dragons collect for their beds are found underground, guarded by the water spirits who enchant them. The spirits enchant these jewels to destroy pure evil."

"What about the pirates?" asked Ethan, "How come they can they steal them?"

"They're bad men, but not pure evil, so it won't kill them. However, the longer they hold on to the jewels, the more it eats away at the evil inside them. Have you ever smelled one of them?" the man asked.

"Yeah! Penny's new boyfriend smelled awful," Ethan said.

"Shut up, Ethan. How do the dragons get the jewels?" Penny asked, changing the subject.

"They have a keen sense of smell and can sniff out the underground mines. The water spirits allow them to take the enchanted stones in hopes of keeping worldly peace. It's this enchantment, or magic that not only destroys evil, it also allowed you to open the portal. That was an unexpected discovery. Come on."

He lifted himself to another opening. The cave was deep, and he could see a bed of jewels way in the back but couldn't quite tell if anyone was home or not.

Penny and Ethan climbed up to join him. "I think this might work," he said as he pointed to the pile of jewels.

"Okay, you guys guard the front, and I'll be right back." Penny assumed she would be the one to go, considering herself the fastest, but the man grabbed the back of her dress and insisted he go, since he knew dragons better than either of them. Penny, of course, dug her heels in harder and wouldn't take no for an answer.

"Your stubbornness is very familiar to me." The old man relented. "You go and I'll keep watch. Hurry."

Before Penny could make a move, Ethan took off to the back of the cave.

"Stop!" Penny said in a loud whisper, but it was too late. Ethan was too far into the cave. "What is he thinking?"

Penny and the old man kept their eyes trained to the sky, making sure the homeowner wasn't about to show up. Moments later, Ethan returned with jewel in hand. Penny and the old man stared blankly at him as he handed it to Penny with a huge smile.

Ethan appeared to be waiting for some praise, but all he continued to receive were blank stares. "What?" No thank you? I got the stone, Come on, let's go."

Penny dryly looked at Ethan. "That's a sapphire. We need an emerald."

"What color are emeralds?" Ethan asked.

"GREEN!" the old man and Penny responded together.

Without a word, Ethan took off for the pile again. This time he returned with an emerald. After tucking both jewels into her boot, the three of them began their descent back down the rocky terrain.

"We got the jewel, and we're almost down the mountain. It wasn't that hard," Ethan said.

"They feel the disturbance," said the old man. "The dragon felt it the minute you picked up the wrong stone. They should be here momentarily. Stealing the jewels wasn't the hard part. Getting away with it will be."

"Are you kidding me? One little stone, and they can feel that it's not on the pile?" Ethan asked as he picked up his pace.

"Yes!" replied the man emphatically.

In the distance they heard a shriek and saw a large form coming toward them.

"Great, now everyone knows we're here," Penny said. "Move your butt, Ethan." Penny encouraged him to speed up by pressing the sole of her boot into the top of his head.

They picked up some speed but started slipping, and each of them took turns losing their foothold against the rocks. Penny realized as the dragon eyed her with a beady black stare that it knew she had the stolen goods. It circled above them and swooped down for the kill, as if it was sliding down the mountain, wings tucked back in full-attack mode. At the last split second, Penny jumped, just as the talons uncoiled to impale her. Ethan and the old man gasped as they watched her fall, but she stretched her arm and grabbed a lone branch protruding out from the side of the mountain.

"Don't worry. I planned that," she called up to them.

Flying back into the sky to launch a second attack, the dragon did a 180-degree turn above their heads. They were still about twenty feet up the mountainside. Scurrying like frightened rabbits, they skittered down halfway. Jumping the last ten feet, they avoided the Chuvashia's strike.

Buzz and Laci heard Penny yell, "Run!"

They threw the dried grass in their hands onto the fire and followed the order.

"Another dragon is trying to kill us. I'm getting sick of this," Buzz said as they ran toward the safety of the Yggdrasill tree.

CHAPTER TWENTY-ONE

HEADING SOUTHWEST, IT WAS a direct shot for the Yggdrasill tree. Running at top speed, they tried to avoid getting picked off by a dragon. They zigzagged like a bunch of roaches when the kitchen light goes on. Laci and Buzz, however, had to run in straight lines to catch up with the other three.

As the old man looked back, he observed aloud, "The dragons have retreated to the caves and don't appear to be pursuing us." That news allowed the group to take their sprint down a notch, enabling Buzz and Laci to catch up.

He kept looking behind them suspiciously and commented as to how the chase almost never ended until the dragon had control of the jewel again. He then added, "I hope this isn't a new ambush tactic."

"Neat," Ethan said as he gasped for breath.

As they continued under clear skies, it appeared the attack was over. Quietly and cautiously, they maintained a brisk pace, attempting to keep as low and inconspicuous as possible.

Never leaving silence alone for too long, Buzz started talking as they jogged. "Hey, buddy."

No one responded.

"Hey you. Old guy!"

The man's head snapped around to look at Buzz. "What did you say?"

Buzz looked a little frightened. "Uh, I was just wondering what we should call you. I don't know your name, and I called you *old guy,* which got your attention, but you didn't seem to like it."

The old man looked back at Buzz then panned his gaze across the others. In response to their young faces, his voice softened a little, and he told them, "Call me Verge."

The group returned to traveling in silence, constantly checking the sky to see if their newfound freedom would be short lived or not, but for the moment, it look promising.

Without the constant threat of death, Ethan began speaking. "Excuse me, Verge, but don't you have your own journal? Now that we've got the jewel, what do we need the other one for?"

Laci felt a bit daft for not having asked that question herself. "He's right. Can't we use yours to get home?" Out of her peripheral vision, she saw Ethan gloating over thinking of something before she did.

"I'm afraid it's not that simple. This journal..." He tapped his coat pocket. "...unlike your journal, hasn't been enchanted. The water spirits are stingy when it comes to handing out enchantments to humans, since humans tend to misuse power."

Looking frustrated, Ethan shook his head and began to mumble to himself. "Water spirits, of course. What an idiot I am. Why didn't I think of that? Everyone knows that water spirits don't go throwing out enchantments all willy-nilly. I mean, if we could find a magical troll... or maybe a fairy could sprinkle some dust on it, then maybe I could go home."

"Then we're not the only people who have a journal?" asked Laci.

Verge smiled at her and said, "There's something special about you, isn't there? You're correct, young lady. You kids are not the only travelers I've met."

Verge picked up the pace again and put some distance between them, ending the conversation. Then he stopped in his tracks, turned to face them, and asked, "Why did you open the portal? And how did you know how to open it?" He singled out Laci with his questions.

"Well, I... I didn't mean to open a portal. I just found the page with the outline of the emerald and wanted to see if that was the exact outline, and of course it was. Then I read the words underneath it. And I guess that's how it opened."

Verge looked flabbergasted. "How could you do that?"

"It was an accident." Laci shrunk back.

"No, I don't mean it that way. I'm not angry. I mean, you wouldn't know how to read Norn. It's a dead language." Verge pulled out his journal, flipped to a page, and handed his book to Laci. She looked at the scratch marks on the page and wondered how she had managed to turn anything like that into words.

"Holy cow!" Buzz leaned over her shoulder to get a better look at the journal. "You can read that? It looks like a bunch of chickens had a fight in the coop and left a big mess. Speaking of that, remember that summer I went to my cousin's farm? I was supposed to stay the entire summer, but they sent me back after three weeks. Though, I guess I'm not supposed to talk about that. My parents and my aunt and uncle told me never to mention it again."

"I don't know how, but it came to me when I held the book. I didn't think it was hard then..." Laci trailed off as she tried to focus her eyes on the words. Her headache was still pounding, but the words slowly came into focus, and she could read them again.

"It found you," Verge whispered to himself.

"See, I told you reading would lead to no good," Ethan jokingly said to Buzz.

Buzz blankly stared back at Ethan.

"Dude, it's a joke."

"Okay, Laci sent us here accidentally, but she couldn't get us back. Why not?" Penny asked.

Verge explained, "You must say the incantation in the language of the land you're traveling to. She would have needed to have translated it to English to get you back."

"But that baby dragon came to us when she read the chicken scratch! We didn't go there first." Penny pointed out the obvious flaw in his explanation.

Verge continued. "That's because the universe must always be in balance. When one thing enters, another must leave. You actually sent someone here, and the baby dragon was merely keeping the balance."

Laci thought aloud, "The baby dragon must have wandered to the knoll, which is why the mother was searching for it there."

"But then who came here to get Digger to show up in the attic?" Buzz asked.

"Fluffy!" Penny shrieked. "She was up in the attic with us, and then I couldn't find her after the fire."

Verge looked confused, so Penny clarified, "Fluffy is a cat."

"Well then, if that's the case, I have a scary question," Ethan chimed in. "Who replaced the four of us and the baby dragon when we came here? Did we send five dragons or styggs or witches or pirates to the garage?" As they discussed this frightening prospect, they arrived at the Yggdrasil tree.

Climbing over the enormous roots was tiring, but the tree protected them from any hungry dragons that might be looking for a mid-morning snack or searching for a stolen jewel.

Laci's eyesight was failing her again, but her hearing was fine. "You guys, I hear something." She pressed her ear against a root. Other than a few large ant-looking things headed for her face, she didn't detect anything. She hurdled over more roots, periodically putting her ear near them, trying to figure out where the noise had come from. A moaning sound echoed below them.

"I hear it now, too," said Penny. They all searched for the source of the noise.

"It's coming from down here." Laci found some tangled tree roots creating a gap, which allowed her to peer below. She could make out a pool of water. It dawned on her that in legends, the Well of Wisdom was below the Yggdrasill tree. Or this could merely be a place where rainwater gathered after it rained. She wiggled the top half of her body through some of the roots.

"Laci, where are you going?" Penny asked.

"I see something. It looks like someone is sitting in the corner."

"Laci?" the voice called out.

"Hallvard?" She was overjoyed to hear his voice but soon realized that he was lying on the ground in a pool of something dark. "Are you okay?" she asked, knowing the answer wouldn't be positive.

"This is my punishment for being such a fool. I never should have trusted him. I swear I would have come back for you, on my family's honor."

Laci heard him cough weakly. It sounded like there could be blood in his cough. "Hold on, I'll be right down." She tossed her backpack to Penny for safekeeping and shimmied through the roots.

"Laci!" Penny tried to stop her. "If something attacked him, it could still be down there."

Laci didn't listen and continued to wiggle her way between the roots.

"I'll go with her," Ethan offered, as he wedged his way through behind her. Their thin frames wormed between the thick, black-knotted wood, and they dropped to the hard, damp ground below.

Looking up, a web of roots with sunlight sneaking in canopied over them. "I feel like an ant," Laci said with her eyes focused on the enormity of their surroundings as she turned to see a maze of tunnels circling them. It was like Grand Central Station for the underground group.

Ethan ran to Hallvard and found he'd been stabbed in the chest and was bleeding extensively. "The paper!" Ethan held out his hand.

"Does he have the journal?" Laci asked.

Ethan looked at Hallvard, who shook his head no in disgrace.

Laci gave Ethan the page, now soaked in blood and a bit gooey and foul.

Ethan grimaced, spread it onto Hallvard's chest, and pressed down.

Hallvard screamed in pain.

"It's not working! Do you have any others? This one must be too dirty," said Ethan.

Laci sat beside Hallvard and gently pressed down on the bloody page, asking him, "Where's the journal?"

He grabbed her hand "Please forgive me. I feel the end is near for me. I am sorry I have failed you."

Laci asked him again.

"Thuban took it," he answered.

"You're not going to die right now. You'll be fine," Laci explained to him as she wadded up the blood-soaked page and shoved it back in her hoodie pocket.

"You have magic, Miss Laci, don't you?" He looked at his bloody chest and patted the area where he had been stabbed. "I feel my strength return." After a few minutes, he was able to stand up.

Verge yelled down, "Hurry up."

As Hallvard gained enough of his balance to walk, Laci had to ask, "Is that really the Well of Wisdom?" She pointed to the large bubbling spring.

"I believe it is," Hallvard responded.

"Here, hold him." Laci leaned Hallvard into Ethan and ran to the well.

Hallvard reached out to grab her, but in his weakened condition, she easily slipped through his grip.

"It is not safe for mortals to drink from the Well of Wisdom," he pleaded with her.

With reckless abandon, she cupped her hands and took a drink of water. As she wiped her mouth with her sleeve, they all stared at each other, wondering if Laci was about to fall over and drop dead. After a few moments, she decided she'd live. "Okay, I'm ready now. Let's go."

Hallvard asked, "Are you sure you feel fine?"

"I feel great. Stop worrying about me." She jumped up to grab one of the tree roots in order to pull herself back through.

"Um, Laci, I don't think that water is working very well. Looks like the exit is that way." Ethan pointed to an incline with a small exit hole to return to ground level.

Just then, a loud rumbling reverberated though the tunnel. Almost knocked to the ground, the three scrambled to stay upright and headed toward the ramp.

"I think we're having an earthquake!" cried Ethan.

"I don't think so," said Laci. "Those sound like steps."

Out of the maze of tunnels, a giant appeared. At ten feet tall, he was forced to walk hunched over to avoid hitting the tangled root ceiling. Each of his labored steps caused clumps of dirt and grass to fall through the gaps from above. He wore a suit of leather armor, and his long black hair cascaded down his back. His physique made it appear as if he could lift the entire tree on his shoulders if he wanted to. For an underground dweller, his skin and hair seem void of dirt, but it was his piercing blue eyes that held their attention.

"It appears you have awoken Mimir by drinking from the well," Hallvard said. "You must sacrifice something to drink from the well, as Odin sacrificed one of his eyes for the knowledge."

"WHAT?" shrieked Laci. Then she thought about the legend. "Wait, I thought Mimir was decapitated by the Vanir and his head sent back to Odin?"

Mimir blocked their escape route and continued to approach them.

"Apparently not," Hallvard pointed out. "He's still here." The three backed up at the same rate Mimir advanced.

"I'm sorry. I forgot about the rules," Laci called out to the giant. She looked at Hallvard. "Does he understand me?"

Hallvard shrugged as he wielded his dagger yet again.

Laci fished through her pockets, not wanting to sacrifice an eye or ear or anything of that sort. At the bottom of her pocket, she found her house key. The keychain had a small flashlight attached to it. Quickly, she removed the key and extended her arm with the flashlight on her palm. "Here, will you please accept this in exchange for the water I drank? It's from the future, sort of. It's something you don't have right now. It'll give you more wisdom in your well."

Plastering a smile on her face, she mentally crossed her fingers that the ridiculous trade would work, and she approached the giant. His long straggly hair swayed with each labored step as he moved closer to meet her. She held up the flashlight and showed him how to push the little button and make it light up. When the light turned on, it flashed in his face and startled him, causing him to jump up and bump his head on a root, letting out a boisterous yell.

Laci cowered. "I'm so sorry, again."

As he rubbed his head, she attempted the demonstration again but aimed the flashlight away from him. She gingerly held it out and dropped it into his enormous hand. "Gently. Press the button gently, or it'll break."

She thought about his size and how he'd probably crush it to pieces as soon as he touched it. Then what the heck could she use for a trade?

He pressed the button and it lit up. "Trick?" he asked.

Laci shook her head. "May we pass you and leave please?"

Mimir studied the flashlight and apparently decided it was a good enough trade. He moved aside to allow them to pass. As they walked up the ramp of roots, Laci turned back to see Mimir throw the flashlight into the well then disappear down one of the tunnels.

"You had a flashlight with you, Laci? We could have used that in the cave with the witches, ya know? Maybe you should have drunk that smart water on the way there, not the way back," Ethan said.

As they reached the top, Penny, Verge, and Buzz rushed over. "Did you feel that earthquake?" Penny asked.

"Feel it? We saw it," Ethan responded.

When Penny saw Hallvard, she asked, "What's he doing here, and where's our journal and emerald?"

Hallvard hung his head. "I am so sorry for my actions. Please let me explain. At the village where we had our midday meal, Thuban asked questions about you. I knew you had mysteriously traveled here and had that book which was somehow connected. So I told him about it. Later he told me that Penny kept a jewel in her boot, which we would need as well."

Verge stopped his story. "Why does he want the journal? What's he going to do with it?"

Hallvard shook his head. "I never knew he wanted it at all. When I spoke of seeking revenge if I could find the twin dragons at the caves, he said he wished to find the dragons, too. He remembered the wars well and promised to send me through the time machine to save my father."

Buzz interrupted, "There's a time machine? That's so cool."

Penny's jaw dropped at Buzz's inability to follow along. "The portal, Buzz. Remember going through the portal?"

Not giving up, Buzz said, "But he said time machine."

Penny gave him a glare to shut him up that lasted for a good half hour.

"Come on, we have to stop him," Verge said as he quickly moved them along.

"But I don't know where he has taken it," Hallvard said as he followed.

"We do," said Laci.

CHAPTER TWENTY-TWO

WITH NO TIME TO waste, they took off. Verge wasn't the friendliest guy she'd ever met, but, after the past few days, Penny wasn't afraid of much. "What's the plan?" she asked.

"I'll tell you when we get there," said Verge.

Before she could get him to elaborate, she saw him pointing to something in front of them. Another of those horrid styggs appeared, and it was coming straight for her.

Hallvard raced forward with dagger in hand, eyes set on killing the stygg and saving Penny, but his plan was thwarted as he lunged toward it and slipped on a rock, losing his balance. The dagger flew into the air and landed in the dirt, well out of his reach. Hallvard's hasty retreat reflexes failed him, and the stygg clipped his leg. He was knocked down, and his face slammed against the ground.

"That was almost comical, but Hallvard, we're depending on you to kill these things," Ethan said as he moved nearer to Penny.

The creature circled them after making its first strike. Buzz was closest to the dagger.

"Quick, Buzz, pick it up!" Penny yelled at him.

The stygg honed in on Buzz's movement as he clumsily stumbled toward the dagger. In a panicked scurry to avoid the creature, he accidentally kicked the dagger farther away into some tall grass and out of sight.

"Genius" was all Penny could say.

Looking for a new target, it aimed its attention on Laci. Darting toward her, it grunted and snarled, racing through the small grass.

She took off her backpack and swung it as hard as she could, managing to smack the creature upside the head. It looked a little like a sinking ship listing to the left, as it shook the hit off.

"Nothing quite like taking volume one of the entire English literary collection to the side of your head," Penny said to congratulate Laci on her quick thinking.

Without warning, it jerked to the right and knocked Ethan to the ground, pinning him under its weight.

Penny ran over and kicked the thing so hard upside its head it fell over completely.

"Goal!" Buzz yelled with his arms in the air.

Penny leaned down to help Ethan up. "Looks like I had to save you twice today."

Ethan stood and gave Penny a sly smile as he brushed the dirt and leaves off him.

They soon learned that styggs were stubborn creatures, and this one was no exception. It got up and fell down several times until it finally ran into the forest in, unfortunately, the same direction they needed to go.

Hallvard found his dagger after several minutes of searching and returned to the group with a humble smile. "Ready now."

After making it across the remaining tall grass and reaching the edge of the forest, Verge handed out jerky to everyone and searched for leaves with pooled-up rainwater to drink.

While eating their jerky, Laci approached Hallvard. "What exactly do the legends say about people dropping dead after drinking from the Well of Wisdom?"

"I have heard that mere mortals will immediately turn to dust. I guess you are no mere mortal."

Laci beamed for a moment then asked, "Have you heard any other legends about random people drinking from the well and what it did for them? I'm wondering what I might end up with after trading a mini-flashlight. I'm hoping it's not a shortened lifespan."

Hallvard shook his head while he finished the last of his jerky. As he turned toward Verge to get moving again, Laci began poking herself.

"What are you doing?" he asked.

"Just seeing if anything lights up on me. You don't see anything flashing, do you?" She kept poking and talking to herself. "I don't see anything glowing, but I can see. I mean, I can really see. Everything is astonishingly clear." Laci skipped to catch up to the others as she said to herself, "Monumental!"

Hallvard turned his head as she caught up. "Are you okay?"

"Never been better."

As good as things were going for Laci, Penny couldn't shake the dread she felt. She knew it was impossible to avoid traveling through the vines she'd found so disagreeable the day before.

Hallvard chopped at shrubbery to create a path when Verge grabbed his arm. "Wait!" he cautioned.

Ethan leaned over and said to Buzz under his breath, "What's the matter? Was he about to step into Laci's dung heap?"

Buzz could barely speak through his giggles. "I think I can still smell it." Laughing at his zinger, neither noticed the evil eye Laci threw their way.

Looking around on the ground, she found a pinecone and pegged Ethan square in the head.

"Ouch!" Ethan was caught completely off guard by her accuracy and strength, responding only with his gaped mouth gawk.

She smiled at both of them. "There's something else I got from that water. You know, Ethan, my vision is so clear right now, I could see your tiny little—"

Clearly unaccustomed to fourteen-year-old behavior, Verge interrupted their banter. "We're about to enter a dangerous area."

"You mean the dragons and everything else we've faced haven't been dangerous?" Buzz asked.

"The vines act as if they have a mind of their own. You must avoid them."

Penny scoffed and pulled up her tattered skirt, revealing her wound from the vine. "Been there, done that. Don't worry, we discovered them the hard way." She acted confident but wasn't feeling secure about reentry.

Verge led them into the thick of the forest.

"But wait, we should be headed that way." Penny pointed in a different direction, one farther south. "That's how we came on our way out here." Penny had always been proud of her sense of direction. No matter what city she was in, if she had travelled the route before, she could always find her way back. This skill came in handy when she and her mom had taken road trips together.

"We're headed toward Botkyrka, right?" Verge asked.

Penny nodded.

"Then we go this way."

Penny turned her gaze to Hallvard, who immediately spun around and followed Verge. "You took us on a few detours on our way to the caves, didn't you?"

"Hey, Laci," Ethan called back to her, "you might want to get your boyfriend a GPS for Christmas this year."

Laci didn't respond and was falling behind.

Penny slowed her pace to walk next to her friend.

"I'm a little uncomfortable right now," Laci whispered to Penny. "After drinking from the well, then from the leaves, followed by pressing on all parts of myself, including my stomach, to check for light, my hamster bladder is ready to split. There's absolutely no way I want any of them to know I need a bathroom stop."

Penny nodded. "Make it quick. I don't want to fall too far behind."

Laci squatted behind the nearest bush, looking down to make sure a backpack strap wasn't going to get hit. A glowing puddle formed below her. She called out, "Penny, come quick!" Pulling her shorts back on, she kept staring at the puddle.

"What is it?" Penny asked as she approached.

"Just look." Laci pointed to the puddle.

Penny turned her gaze and was amazed. "What is it?"

"My pee. I think the well water made it all funky." Laci gritted her teeth.

"I'll say." Penny looked to see how far behind they were. "I'd love to stay and chat about it, but we'd better catch up with the others."

Laci followed her. "Penny, I think it helped my vision, but what if I pee it out?"

Penny stopped. "Laci, don't pee again. Listen to me. I know you can't hold more than a Dixie cup, but you've got to keep that in you until we get home. I need you to be able to see at your best."

Laci nodded, and they ran to catch up to the others.

"Where have you been?" Ethan asked as he turned to see what the scuffle behind him was.

"Female problems." Penny knew that nothing would shut down an eighth-grade boy quicker than that answer.

The girls ran past them to catch up to Verge. "How much longer?" Penny asked.

"Not much." This was the typical no-nonsense answer Penny had expected from Verge.

More rustling could be heard behind them. Ethan casually looked back but soon realized everyone was in front of him. "That hyena on steroids is back!" Ethan ran forward as Hallvard passed him going in the opposite direction.

As the stygg bore down, Hallvard dove at it again, but he didn't get a clean strike. The wounded animal was clearly angry and still seemed a bit disoriented from its recent kick to the head. It snarled wildly, thrashing its tusks back and forth. As the group moved, they noticed the vines moved now, too.

"They know we're here," Verge told the group. "Don't touch them."

As they stumbled over their own feet trying to avoid the vines, the creature charged again, causing them to run in different directions. "Stay together!" Hallvard and Verge both yelled, but it was too late; they had separated.

Laci attempted to circle back but got tangled when a vine grabbed her backpack. She pulled to get it free, while a lower vine wrapped itself around her foot. She screamed for help.

Penny sprinted over. The four legged creature locked on and took off after her.

Hallvard intercepted and managed to stab it again, but it was too strong for him to keep down for long.

Penny reached Laci, who'd become more entangled in the angry vines. As soon as Penny began to pull on the vine around Laci's foot, it released its grip. She then pulled the other vines off one by one. Laci was set free and stumbled forward, but the stygg caught sight of her, broke from Hallvard's hold, and charged again. Hallvard lunged out in an attempt to stab it, but it was out of his reach.

"Get behind the tree!" Penny ordered Laci.

Following her instructions, Laci did just that. The stygg charged at Penny. With the vines still in her hands, she waited until the stygg was about to strike her, juked to the side, and dropped the vines onto its back. Immediately they tightened and yanked it up to the lower branch of its host tree, twisting around the beast until it could no longer move. As the vines tightened, the animal squealed in pain.

Hallvard plunged his dagger into its chest and pulled down with all his might, ripping the suffering animal in half. The winding intestines spilled onto the ground, and the thick purple blood oozed down around them. The beast went silent.

"Is that a license plate?" Buzz pointed as the stomach contents landed at their feet. Going in for a closer look, they saw it wasn't a license plate, but a book. "Hey, Laci, I think this might be one of your books."

Laci ran over to get a better look. She started to stick her hand into the gory mess, but Verge grabbed her arm and pulled her back. "We don't have time."

Following his lead, she ran off, leaving behind the mess and her chance to redeem herself at the library.

Climbing a hill at a break in the woods, they spotted the woodshed and knew that just beyond that they would reach the knoll. Approaching the shed, they saw Thuban with the journal and jewel in his gloved hand, but they stopped in their tracks when they saw he was in the middle of a battle with the two pirates they had dealt with the day before.

"This is our chance to get the journal back. Come on!" said Verge as he ran toward the action.

Thuban toyed with the pirates. His fearless style showed his combat experience. He casually held his sword in one hand and the jewel and journal in the other. He swatted away the pirates, their swords sporadically made contact with him and on a few occasions drew blood, but he remained focused on trying to open the portal. Spinning around, he knocked one of the pirates over and caught a glimpse of the group heading up the knoll.

The pirates turned to see the group advancing on them. With their attention distracted, it gave Thuban the necessary time he needed to read the journal aloud and open the vortex. Scared by the glowing orb, the pirates retreated from the hill.

His cold unflinching stare didn't deter Verge from charging up the hill as fast as he could, but before Verge reached him, Thuban stepped into the swirling transport. The orb closed before Verge could follow him through.

Thuban was gone, and in his place was a large grey rat, its tail still smoldering from the trip. It looked at Verge with its beady black eyes, let out a loud squeak, and ran off.

"No!" Verge yelled. "We have to stop him." As he turned to the group, the two sword-wielding pirates approached him.

He backed up toward the woodshed, when the taller pirate spotted Penny. "Hey, Slim, your girlfriend's back." The short fat smelly pirate changed direction and moved toward Penny.

"Protect her!" Hallvard shouted. Ethan picked up a large stick and got between them. Buzz ran around in a circle and, not finding anything in the immediate vicinity, picked up a handful of dirt.

Ethan looked over at Buzz. "That's all you got?"

Buzz shrugged.

Hallvard ushered Penny and Laci into the woodshed just as Verge arrived and followed them in. "Keep the girls safe," he said to Verge as he returned to the pirates.

Verge rubbed his face in his hands. "The journal is gone. I failed."

"Not all of it." Laci pulled the bloody wadded mess out of her pocket.

Verge eyed it with a healthy dose of skepticism. "I don't think it's going to be enough, but we can try." He opened it and flattened it on the dirt floor of the woodshed. "I can't use this; I need to be able to write the incantation on it. There's no space. Plus, the page is too wet from the blood."

Laci opened her backpack. "I have something else that might work." She removed the note that Hallvard had written her. It was in pristine condition.

"Yes, this is perfect!" Verge pulled a pencil out of his jacket pocket and started to scribble on the back of the note. He pulled his own journal out to make sure everything was correct. "The jewel." He put his hand out, and Penny retrieved the emerald from her boot and handed it to him. "Now we need to get to the top of that knoll. There isn't enough power here to open the portal.

"You need more bars?" Penny asked as she peeked out the door to see if the coast was clear. Hallvard was gallantly dueling the taller pirate, while Ethan and Buzz were hitting the short smelly one with a stick and throwing dirt into his face. Ethan hauled off with all his might and swatted the pirate in the head, knocking him down. The rotund pirate tried to get back up and grab his sword, but stumbled and fell just as Buzz hit him in the face with a giant dirt clod. Buzz grabbed the sword, but the weight of it caused him to fall over. Ethan took it away before Buzz hurt himself.

"It's clear. Let's go," Penny said to Verge and Laci. As they exited the woodshed, running for the top of the knoll, Penny motioned for Ethan and Buzz to follow. They sprinted up the hill with the smelly pirate in pursuit.

"Start reading it," Verge said to Laci.

"But we're not at the top," Laci said.

"Close enough. Read it now!" he shouted.

Laci focused on the page while running. The words began to form from the lines, and she started to translate them, but it was as if someone forgot to pay the electric bill. The lines came in and out. "I can't quite see it," Laci said as she squinted at the page.

"Did you pee?" Penny asked.

"No!" Laci yelled. "It's weak. The signal here is weak."

"It's the page," Verge explained. "It's not powerful enough."

Meanwhile, the smelly pirate was almost on them. "They have another emerald!" he yelled to the other.

"Oh, come on, Laci," Ethan encouraged her. "Hurry up."

Just as it became clear, a yell broke her concentration. The smelly pirate reached them and wanted his sword back from Ethan. Laci, however, looked right past him and glimpsed Hallvard easily handling the other pirate.

He saw her and yelled over, "You can do this."

She looked back at the paper. The words were there, and she began to translate them into English. Verge tripped the pirate before he reached Ethan, causing the pirate to slam into the ground.

"Toss me the sword," Verge ordered Ethan, who complied.

As Laci finished reading the passage, the vortex appeared, but it was much smaller and not as bright as the one they'd traveled through before.

Penny grabbed Ethan's arm, and he grabbed Buzz. Buzz tried to grab Verge, but Verge had pinned the pirate to the ground, out of reach.

The vortex sucked the three toward it, but Penny held them back. "Not without Laci."

Laci had been concentrating so hard on the paper that she hadn't moved into the vortex. Penny reached out, grabbed her, and yanked her in. All four were sucked through like a funhouse mirror. As the vortex closed, four little confused looking kittens sat in a cardboard box replacing the kids.

Verge stood, releasing the pirate, staring at the box of kittens. Hallvard turned to look at the knoll, now vacant of his new friends.

The pirates slowly walked away without any treasure. Then Verge ran down the hill, screaming at the top of his lungs, wielding the sword over his head, and they sprinted toward the forest and disappeared into the trees.

CHAPTER TWENTY-THREE

THE JOURNEY BACK THROUGH the Pixy Stix expedition wasn't quite the same as the first time. It could have had something to do with the direction they traveled or the fact that they only had the one page to get power from, but this time it felt more like being stuck in a taffy-pulling machine, stretching them from all different directions. Once they took off on their portal journey, it was impossible to steer the ship, so they were left to the mercy of the universe as to where they ended up. On the trip out, they disembarked on top of a nice grassy knoll. However, being unable to leave from that exact spot, they couldn't be sure where they were going to land.

The ride came to an end, and they found themselves crammed inside some sort of box. A slight residual smoke created the effect of steam trapped in there with them, making it difficult at first to figure out where they were. Jammed together like sardines, they could barely move.

Buzz's face was squished against glass. "This tastes salty," he said as he painfully tried to shut his mouth, but it was pressed in such an awkward position that he couldn't quite squeeze his lips together.

"Where are we?" Laci asked.

"I guess the side of the hill must be in the same plane as Grandma's shower, here in this dimension." Ethan recognized the location, as the shower handle dug into his ribs.

"Could someone please open the door?" Penny asked from the back of the enclosure.

"Who built this, stick people? This has to be the smallest shower in the world," Ethan complained as he reached for the door latch.

Something blocked him.

"Laci's backpack is in my way."

Laci tried to move but couldn't, so Ethan reached under it.

"Hey!" Laci cried out and jumped at the same time. "That's my butt, not the door."

"Well, that was mortifying. Sorry about that. Could you try and turn just a little? I think I can reach the door," Ethan said.

Laci turned slightly but ended up stabbing Buzz with the corner of a book in her backpack.

"OUCH!" he cried out as he struggled to move his arm. "I can't get it either."

Finally, Penny reached from behind, her arm stretched in unnatural positions, snaking around her friends and releasing the latch. The door popped open like a can of biscuits and they oozed out, one by one.

"Grandma?" Penny immediately called out. Her first mission was to make sure her family was okay.

"Shouldn't we be quiet, in case Thuban is here?" Laci asked.

Penny ran out the door.

"I guess she's not afraid of him," Ethan said.

Penny checked each room but soon discovered that no one was home. They passed through the kitchen and Buzz saw a stack of papers on the counter. "Hey, guys, look!" He picked up a page and showed them. "We're missing!"

"Really?" Ethan asked.

"Oh, I guess that was obvious. I'll shut up now." Buzz turned to return the flier to the pile.

"I suppose that answers our question about whether time stopped while we were gone. It was just your crappy phone, Ethan." Penny grabbed the flier before Buzz had a chance to put it down. "They used our school pictures. I hate the way my hair looked."

Laci looked over her shoulder. "I think your hair looks cute. You always look good. It's Ethan who needs to worry about his photo."

"What?" Ethan snatched the flier out of Penny's hand.

Laci and Penny giggled.

"I forgot it was picture day. It's not my fault."

Penny looked at Ethan. "I like the singed tips you've got going now."

Ethan tapped the top of his spiky haircut with his hand and ran for the hall mirror. The trip through the vortex, on top of his recent run-in with Digger's flame breath, had changed his hair tips from bleach-blond to black. He looked in the mirror and said, "I kind of like this." He gave them another good tap, but in doing so, they snapped off and crumbled into dusty broken hair. "Awwwww."

Penny started to laugh. "It was a good look while it lasted. Come on, we have more important things to deal with than hair. Like finding my grandma."

"Yeah, and finding Thuban," Laci added.

They ran down the front steps when her grandma's car pulled into the driveway. Grandma saw them running toward her and quickly got out of the sedan.

Penny reached her first and gave her a huge hug. She couldn't remember having ever been so happy to see her grandmother.

"I'm so glad you kids are all safe. We've been worried sick about you."

Penny hugged Grandma even tighter. "We're fine and glad to be back home." She loosened her grip when her grandmother gasped for a breath.

"Where have you kids been for the last two days? The whole town has been looking for you."

Penny stared blankly at her grandmother. They'd never bothered, or had the time, to discuss what they were going to tell people to explain where they'd been. Nobody would believe a story filled with dragons, man-eating vines, disorienting Glem fog, and a spiny fingered, vicious Anna Sophia Robb.

Buzz started to talk. It wasn't in his usual hyper way, but calm and apologetic. "We're so sorry. It's mainly my fault. I had seen a railcar down at the station. It was empty, and I wanted to check out what it was like inside. I talked them into going with me, and they're all such good friends, they agreed. But once we were in the car, our weight must have tipped it ever so slightly, and that started it rolling a little ways down the track. It picked up speed quickly, and the door closed before we could jump out, but the way it works, the latch locked from the outside. It rolled us down a sidetrack used for storage, and we ended up too far away from the regular station for anyone to hear us yelling. We tried all sorts of ideas to get out of there. Eventually, Penny and Laci figured out how to use a rock and paper to open the door. And that explains why we're so-o-o-o-o hungry right now, since we had absolutely no food in the railcar."

For once in his life, Buzz wasn't quoting something from *Super Paranormal Facts*. This was actually almost believable. After the story set in for a moment, they all nodded.

"Well then..." Grandma took her purse out of the car. "...come into the house, and I'll make you something to eat while you call your parents to let them know you're okay. Oh, I'd better call the police first. They'll want to talk to you too. I hope you don't get in any trouble for trespassing at the rail station." She shook her head and finger at them. "You being mischievous kids, you." She gave Penny another enormous hug and kissed her on the head repeatedly.

The sandwiches were eaten quickly, the phone calls were made, and the parents collected their wayward children. A lively discussion of why they hadn't used their cell phones to call, forced Ethan to relive the pain of his busted iPhone. Surprisingly enough, the parents didn't press their kids for too many details, clearly overjoyed that they were back safe.

After visiting with her mother, Penny asked to spend the evening with her grandmother and was in the kitchen helping her clean up the dishes from lunch. Her journey was still vivid in her mind, but so was the guilt of turning her family's world upside-down.

"I'm so sorry. I didn't mean to ruin your wedding. It was an accident," Penny said to her grandmother. Even though they'd lied and hadn't spent a second in that railcar, traveling through the vortex and getting trapped in another realm was technically still an accident.

Grandma looked at her. "I know you are. It's okay, dear, Pastor Jenkins said he would open up any day we needed for the wedding, even if it means moving the bingo tournament."

Penny smiled and gave her grandma another hug. "I guess it makes sense since you helped build that church," she said as she dried another dish.

"Oh, that wasn't really me. I was just a little girl then. It was my parents. They wanted a church in town. I hope one day when you get married, you have your wedding there, too."

The week passed quietly and without incident. Grandma convinced Pastor Jenkins to move the wedding to the following Sunday. Since everything had been ready to go the week before, the townspeople kicked in and got it all back on track for that Sunday. Another benefit of living in a small town was how often the community came together in the face of a crisis.

Another crisis was that Penny's bridesmaid dress was a disaster beyond repair. She and Laci decided to use the remaining intact pieces of it to make a decorative pillow for her grandma as a wedding gift. Penny designed it, while Laci did the lion's share of the sewing.

Laci spent that night with Penny at her grandmother's, which allowed them to relive the adventure and dissect every detail of their trip. Laci brought most of their conversations full circle as to how wonderful Hallvard was. Penny liked the fact that Laci's mind was out of her fantasy books and actually involved in reality, even if that reality lived in another realm.

Their weeklong quest to find Thuban yielded no results. No sign of him appeared anywhere in town. Every morning they took long walks, looking for clues to his whereabouts, or what he might be up to, but they came up empty. The quest to find Thuban, getting ready for the wedding, along with checking the attic, garage, and shower regularly for dragons, kept the girls busy and made the time fly by.

Saturday night before the wedding, Laci sat in Penny's room at her grandmother's, helping her finish the pillow, theorizing what might have happened to Thuban.

"Maybe he never made it," Penny hopefully suggested. "We don't know how accurate it is. I mean, we ended up in the shower. Maybe he ended up in the sewer pipe or something."

The thought of Thuban hunched over in a ball, stuck in a sewer pipe made them laugh.

"Yeah, or maybe he ended up in a garbage truck." Both girls giggled.

"He did have kind of a weird smell," Penny pointed out.

"I wonder if he was a fugitive and needed to escape his land?" Laci asked.

"Well, we know he's a thief."

Laci grabbed her backpack and pulled out the box from the attic and opened it. All the other artifacts were still in there. "I wonder if these are for traveling to the different realms that Verge talked about," she pondered.

"You don't really want to go through that vortex again, do you?" Penny looked at Laci, who smiled back and shook her head, but they both knew she did. Without the journal, however, it was irrelevant.

CHAPTER TWENTY-FOUR

IT WAS THE DAY of Grandma's wedding. Penny wore a simple champagne-colored dress, which erased the memory of the pink poufy disaster, and left her looking like she'd stepped off the cover of *Vogue* once again. Laci had borrowed one of Penny's hand-me-down dresses, so she, too, looked prettier than usual. Around her neck hung a beautiful emerald necklace. Penny added some lose curls in Laci's hair, giving it a summer beach look. As she glanced into the mirror, Laci smiled and said, "If only Hallvard could have seen me look like this, instead of wearing my hoodie."

The girls headed down the stairs and witnessed the chaos that was her grandmother's house. Penny's mom was doing some last-minute cooking in the kitchen. Three women from Elsie's bridge group were helping her get ready and trying to calm her nerves. Penny had never seen her grandmother frazzled.

She reached out and grasped her grandma's hand. "It's going to be great."

Just a little encouragement from her granddaughter seemed to help soothe Elsie's nerves.

The front door opened. Ethan and Buzz were dressed in suits and ready to help out any way they could. Ethan had gotten his haircut for the occasion and added mini black-frosted tips to his hair. This extra attention to detail didn't go unnoticed by Penny.

"Hi, Buzz. Hi, Ethan. You guys look good."

While she said "you guys," she never took her eyes off Ethan.

"So do you Penny," Ethan said with a smile.

Penny looked over at Buzz and asked, "Buzz, what do you have in your jacket lapel?"

Buzz beamed with pride as he patted his jacket. "It's a jarfalla leaf. I brought some along, just in case we ever need them again."

"Can you help us by grabbing some of these boxes and taking them to the car?" Penny asked as she smiled at her crazy friend.

Ethan picked up the box filled with centerpieces for the reception. Penny noticed something sticking out of his pocket. "What's that?" she asked as she pointed at it.

Ethan reached in and pulled out his broken cell phone. The pieces of the phone were still in the waterproof case. "It still works, sort of," he said, "though you have to be careful not to cut yourself while you text."

"Are you kidding me? That thing still works?" Penny said.

Laci looked over at Ethan and said, "I guess my mom is right. They don't make things as well as they used to." She smiled at her own joke. "Oh, and Ethan, you'll need to apologize to Hallvard now, since he didn't really break it."

Ethan replied, "Okay, I'll tell him next time I see him." He and Buzz high fived each other and took the boxes out to the car.

They arrived at the church. Grandma's car was packed with kids and supplies for the wedding and reception. Once it was all unloaded, the chapel looked lovely. Flowers and gauze ribbons adorned the ends of the pews and the altar. The soft neutral colors gave a feeling of purity and calm. After being both baptized and married the first time there, Grandma felt a special connection to the church. Penny did too.

The ceremony started, and Penny walked her grandmother to the altar. It appeared the entire town had come for the celebration. The pews were packed. Penny stood beside her as a bridesmaid. She'd been dreading this wedding but now considered it an honor to stand there with such a widely loved woman. She didn't feel silly, like she had been afraid she would. Instead, she felt happy to be home with her loving family and friends. The new dress her mother had bought for her made her feel elegant as well.

Roy stood facing Grandma with a satisfied look. Penny suddenly wished she had made more of an effort to get to know this man. He'd be with her grandma all the time — all the time that Penny used to spend with her.

As she turned a little to smile at Laci, who sat with Buzz and Ethan, she noticed one of the chapel doors slowly creak open. The light coming through washed out the figure sneaking in. She watched as the shape moved along the back and then down the side of the church, slipping into the pew behind her friends. She thought it must be Mr. Stevens, her English teacher. He was always late for class, especially after lunch. Rumor was he would take a nap after he ate, but the teachers got sick of his snoring and stopped waking him up to get to class on time.

"Penny, dear!" Penny shook herself out of her daydream as she realized Grandma had called her name a few times to hold the flowers while they exchanged rings. She concentrated on the flowers to avoid messing up again, and then thought of how delighted she was to see so much happiness on her grandma's face.

"Can you guys smell that?" Buzz whispered to Laci and Ethan.

"Shhhh…" Laci shushed him.

"No, I mean it," Buzz persisted.

"Nobody farted. Now shut up," Ethan snapped at him. "You're going to get us into trouble. Don't embarrass Penny."

Buzz sniffed the air, but the other two ignored him.

Laci was physically at the wedding, but Penny could see the dreamy look on her friend's face and knew her mind was off in Botkyrka. All the romance of the wedding must have had her thinking about Hallvard. Penny smiled at her BFF and turned back to focus on the ceremony.

Abruptly, a voice behind Laci interrupted her daydream, whispering in a raspy tone, "I couldn't have planned a more perfect ending myself."

Laci froze then turned her head slightly to see Buzz and Ethan, who both look petrified. Sitting directly behind them was Thuban. Apparently, the trip through the portal and his week in their realm hadn't been easy on him; he was tattered from head to toe. Laci and the boys were paralyzed in their seats.

The ceremony finished up with the kissing of the bride, but before the pastor could say "I now present to you Mr. and Mrs. Roy Rastaban," Laci was out of her seat and racing up the aisle.

She ran right past the happy couple and whispered into Penny's ear, "Thuban is here!"

Penny's pulse quickened, but she knew this was no time to panic. She immediately ushered all the guests to the outdoor reception behind the chapel. "Okay, everyone, we have hors d'oeuvres outside with drinks and dancing. Let's get a move on and get this party started," she said as she shoved Roy and her grandmother down the aisle.

Grandma turned and gave her a stern look. "Heavens to Betsy, child. What are you doing?"

Penny smiled a fake grin and said nothing.

"What do we do?" Laci asked. "I don't have my backpack here. It's at home."

"Where is he?" Penny asked. As Laci pointed, she realized he was gone, and so were the boys.

"What in blue blazes is going on here?" Roy demanded an answer.

"You have to trust us. Protect yourselves. There's a dangerous guy who followed us here," Penny tried to explain.

"He's got a sword," Laci added, "and he used it to try and kill one of our friends."

"What are you talking about? Is this a joke?" Grandma asked.

Penny stared at her apologetically.

"You didn't really get trapped in a railcar, did you?" She looked Penny in the eye.

"No," Penny admitted. The weight of having lied to her grandmother lifted, but she didn't feel any better. "But please believe me when I say you have to run and hide. He's dangerous."

"Who is this, and why is he here?" Roy grasped Penny's arm.

"I don't know why he's here. I think he may be after us, but I don't know why. His name is Thuban."

Roy turned away from her and searched the church. "Where is he?" he yelled.

"We don't know. He was just here." Laci pointed to where Thuban had been sitting, but the church was apparently empty except for the four of them.

From behind a long curtain, Thuban rolled out facing Roy and, in a high singsong voice, said, "I found you!"

Roy froze in his tracks.

Penny spotted Ethan and Buzz hiding in the back of the church.

"Run, Roy!" Penny shouted. "He's evil."

"Evil? No. I'm not evil," Thuban hissed as he walked closer to Roy. They stared at each other, each at opposite ends of a pew. "I just do what's in my nature."

As he said this, Thuban rushed toward Roy.

Penny and Laci screamed.

Flames shot from underneath him as Thuban approached. The two men collided, causing a blinding flash of light. Both yelled in pain as they swelled in their clothes. Seams tore apart, and black scales with a bluish hue appeared underneath. United again, the two morphed into enormous Chuvashia dragons.

"Brother!" Thuban cried from his transforming face.

"I have been waiting for you!" Roy responded.

Their clothes tore completely off and fell to the ground as the huge bodies filled the church, crushing rows of pews around them. Their heads reached all the way to the rafters of the church.

Laci said to Penny, "Hallvard was wrong. Rau is actually two twin dragons, not just one."

"Oh yeah, I forgot to tell you. Verge told me that at the caves," said Penny.

When Thuban's tattered coat slid down his ridged back and hit the wooden floor, it made a thud.

That sound got Laci's attention. She dropped to the floor and crawled between the pews and the debris. Once she reached the jacket, she dug into the pocket and found what she was looking for: the journal. She patted the coat down and checked the other pockets for the emerald but couldn't find it.

"Wow, they didn't even have to swallow a rock," Buzz observed of Thuban and Roy's transformation as the boys snuck from their hiding place in an attempt to exit the chapel.

The dragons heard them and turned to see where the noise was coming from.

"Run!" Penny yelled. They took her advice and headed for safety. Penny and Laci grabbed her grandmother, who was frozen in fear, and hid behind where the choir sat, while the boys hid under some pews near the back of the church.

Laci whispered to Penny, "They can only die in battle, so we have to fight them."

"With what?" Penny asked.

Both dragons turned and looked down the aisle of the church toward the girls.

"Monumental. They really do have great hearing."

Thuban shot flames at them, setting the altar on fire.

Barely audible, Laci whispered to Penny, "I know what we can use to fight them, but we need to distract them and get your grandma outside."

"Okay, I'll distract them, and you take my grandma out." Penny immediately got up and ran toward the back of the church. Both dragons turned, and Roy cut her off by jumping over the pews and landing in front of her. Laci took the opportunity and snuck Grandma out the back door to the patio. Outside, the party guests were asking what all the commotion was about inside the church.

"Nothing to worry about. We have it under control." Laci tried to assure them, but it didn't do much good. As she headed back in through the side door, she ran past the gift table and spotted the box with the pillow she and Penny had made for Grandma. She ripped it open, grabbed the pillow, tore open a seam, and shoved the journal into it. She threw it back into the box and shut the lid. "We'll save gift opening for much later. I hope dragons don't like to open presents."

When Laci reentered the chapel, she saw both dragons had Penny and the boys cornered. She took a hymnal out of one of the pews. It'd been damaged by the dragon's fire. She held it close to her side.

"Hey! You ever want to see this again, you'd better let my friends go."

Both dragons turned to face her. Thuban opened his mouth as if he was about to turn Laci into a marshmallow on a summer camping trip.

"Don't burn her. She has the journal. We need it to get back home." Roy smacked his brother with his tail.

Thuban closed his mouth. "Why are you still trying to tell me what to do?" he said with disgust.

Roy responded diplomatically, "Well, brother, I know how you like your maiden's fresh. I'd hate to see you burn this one."

"You are right about that, my dear brother. Nothing like fresh maidens." Thuban's monstrous face grinned.

While the dragons were distracted with Laci, Penny noticed the jarfalla leaf sticking out of Buzz's jacket and took it.

"Hey, that's mine." Buzz reached to get it back.

Penny put her finger to her lips to keep him quiet. She rubbed the leaf all over herself.

"Oh, I get it," Buzz whispered. He pulled more jarfalla leaves out of his suit jacket, not just the pocket, but he had torn a hole in the lining and stuffed that with jarfalla leaves as well.

"How many of those did you bring home?" Ethan asked.

The noise drew the attention of the dragons, and they turned and sniffed the air to locate them.

Quickly, Ethan and Buzz rubbed themselves all over with the leaves, then Ethan shoved some into his suit pocket like a handkerchief. They slowly crawled toward Laci, hiding behind the pews as they inched along.

"Where did she go?" Roy said as he turned back to where Laci had been standing.

"You lost her?" Thuban snapped at him.

"I didn't lose her any more than you did. We need to find her and get that journal back."

While they bickered, the kids managed to reunite on the side of the church near the door where they'd hidden Grandma out of sight.

"Let's sneak out this door," whispered Ethan.

"We can't just run from them," said Penny. "If we don't stop them, they will destroy this entire town."

Laci whispered something into Buzz's ear. He nudged Ethan, and they tiptoed out the side door.

Penny was about to stop Ethan when Laci pantomimed part of her plan. Together they peeked out from behind the broken pew rubble only to see two giant dragons staring down at them. They both ran for the door, but Thuban snapped up Laci, and Roy swung his tail at Penny to trip her up then grabbed her off the floor.

CHAPTER TWENTY-FIVE

LACI HAD FANTASIZED THAT one day she would be able to see a dragon up close. This wasn't what she had in mind. This dragon had a personal vendetta against her. His piercing black eyes focused squarely on her as his huge jaws opened. She squirmed and pulled with all her might, but it was useless. She couldn't budge against the strength of this enormous fiend.

"Give me the journal, and I will spare your life and your friends," Thuban said with a hint of sincerity in his voice.

Laci glimpsed a small fire still burning on the floor and tried to throw the hymnal into it, but Roy snatched it out of mid-air. In one hand he held Penny, and in the other he examined the book.

"This isn't the journal. She tried to trick us." Roy threw the hymnal across the church in anger.

"Where is the journal?" Thuban yelled.

Laci said nothing.

"If you don't tell me, I will be forced to bite your head off!" he screamed and tightened his grip.

Laci gulped. She tried to talk but wasn't able to get any words out because she was shaking uncontrollably.

"I-I-I—" Laci stuttered.

"I don't have time for this. Bottoms up." Thuban opened his mouth and dangled her over his head, ready to chomp down.

"No, brother!" Roy warned. While holding Penny in one hand, he pushed his brother with his tail and took Laci away from him. "Don't be so rash. We need that journal to get home. We don't want to get stuck in this realm, trust me."

Thuban spun around to face his brother. "Why do you think you can always tell me what to do, brother? So this little thing hid the book. She is no match for us. It will not take me but a few moments to sniff it out. She could not have gone far with it."

Roy bowed his head in slight submission. Thuban's temper was legendary and had led to their lengthy separation.

"Unless she rubbed the journal in jarfalla leaves, my brother," Roy said.

Laci realized that would have been a great idea and wondered why she hadn't thought of it.

"If any harm comes to me or my friends, you'll never find that book, and you'll be stuck here forever," Laci said with fake confidence.

"Well then, if you don't give me that book. I'm going to start with your friends." Thuban grabbed Penny out of Roy's hand.

"No!" Laci screamed. "I'll tell you. I hid it in the back of the church. Put us down, and I'll show you."

"Let's tie them up while we look for the book. That way we have something to eat for our trip home," Roy said.

"Now that is a plan I can support," Thuban replied.

With his gigantic, clawed hands, Roy quickly tied the girls together with the garlands from the pews. It was wrapped around them so tightly they could barely breathe.

Penny managed to squeeze a few words out. "What's the plan?" she asked in a whisper.

"I just need a little more time," replied Laci.

The dragons tore apart the back of the church, causing the flower arrangements to mess with their sense of smell.

With all the fresh roses, it was hard for them to detect anything else.

"Psst. We're back with what you asked for." Penny and Laci turned to see Ethan and Buzz had silently entered the church and were about ten feet away from them.

"We'll come free you," Ethan said, but Penny and Laci both shook their heads.

"No, don't let them see you," Penny said. "Ethan, give me your phone."

Ethan tossed his baggie-contained cell phone to Penny, who pulled out a piece of the broken plastic and slashed through the garlands, freeing herself and Laci. "Great phone, Ethan!" she said.

The dragons turned back and witnessed the escape attempt.

"Divide and conquer," Laci whispered to Penny.

They each ran in opposite directions. Roy chased Laci, and Thuban ran after Penny. He swiped his claws at her, tearing the new dress and slashing her arm, but she was too fast for him to catch. She rolled under the pews back to Ethan and Buzz. Buzz reached into the other side of his jacket lining. While Ethan rubbed his jarfalla leaf on Penny, Buzz pulled out a mojurt cluster.

"For now, until we can get you Laci's magic paper." Buzz smiled as he dabbed it onto her arm.

Penny and Ethan looked shocked.

"Buzz, you are so prepared!" Penny said.

"What? I like the way they smell," Buzz replied.

Roy chased Laci into the outdoor reception area, causing the wedding guests to flee in mass hysteria.

As Laci ran past the gift table, she noticed that the box hiding the journal was still there and undisturbed. Penny, Ethan, and Buzz followed.

"You guys made me swear not to tell anyone what happened," Buzz complained, "and here we are bringing a couple of angry killer dragons as our date to the wedding. You guys, do you know what this means? I'm gonna get to be on *Super Paranormal Facts!*"

Penny pulled Buzz against her side as they ran. "Focus! We have to help Laci. What did Laci want you to get?"

Ethan opened his jacket, displaying an arsenal of handheld wrist-rocket slingshots. Buzz pulled out his best homemade slingshot, made of surgical tubing and a funnel.

"Awesome. I thought your mom took those away from you," Penny said.

"Oh, she did, but I know where she hides them," Buzz replied.

"Where did Laci go?" Penny asked as she spun her head from side to side, searching.

They looked around but didn't see her, only Roy stomping around the tables. Finally, Penny spotted Laci pressed behind a tree as Roy stalked her.

"Ah, guys," Buzz said as he poked at Ethan's arm then pointed to the sky. Thuban was perched on the roof of the church. His massive weight crushed shingles, which broke off and shattered on the ground.

"Come on!" Penny led them.

Thuban swooped down and landed directly in front of the three of them, preventing them from reaching Laci.

Penny grabbed one of Ethan's wrist-rockets and began firing rocks from the planter at Thuban. Ethan and Buzz followed her lead.

Shooting rocks at the armor of a dragon didn't render great results, but the velocity of the rocks caught Thuban off guard and gave them time to retreat behind the buffet table before he was able to torch them. They continued to fire rocks at him, and a few hit his face, which further irritated him.

"That's not going to work!" Laci yelled from behind a tree.

"Do you have a better idea?" Penny asked.

Laci did, but didn't want to let the dragons know, so she yelled back. "Don't throw the rocks. Throw the *rock*." She dodged Roy's lunge and made a beeline for the buffet table.

Penny said to her, "That's brilliant!"

Both boys looked confused, so Laci quickly gave Buzz and Ethan their instructions.

Thuban sent a fireball toward the buffet table but overshot it and hit the wall behind the gifts. Laci's heart skipped a beat. Thankfully the box hadn't been affected. Thuban turned his head toward the table where she had been looking. Just then, a centerpiece vase filled with flowers pelted Thuban on the side of his head. The shock caused him to change his focus back to his attacker. As he turned, he was hit with another one square in the face. Like Penny, Ethan scooped up the centerpieces and shot them at Roy as fast as he could reload. As Thuban continued to get pelted by glass and flowers, he became visibly more and more angry.

Laci pulled off her emerald necklace and handed it to Buzz, whispering something into his ear, then said loudly, "Don't miss."

Penny saw this interaction and reached for the necklace. "I should take the shot."

Laci grabbed the necklace back and told her, "It has to be Buzz. We can't risk it."

Penny looked confused.

"Trust me. Please," Laci said.

Buzz took quick aim and fired. The jewel soared straight for Thuban, but he saw it coming and snatched it out of the air. The stone burned his hand, and he dropped it. He yanked off a nearby tablecloth, using it to pick the emerald up. Laughing at their attempt to defeat him, he grasped the wrapped-up green jewel in his enormous clawed hand. "Now I have both jewels," he said.

Penny fired anything she could find at Roy — forks, knives, small plates — but nothing seemed to be doing any damage. With lightning fast reflexes, he reached down and scooped her up.

"I never did like you very much," he said to her as he lifted her to his mouth.

Laci ripped Ethan's slingshot out of his hands and loaded it with a lit Sterno tin from the buffet table. She fired the canned heat right into Roy's eye. The condensed liquid alcohol spread across his entire face, blinding him as it burned. Penny fell to the ground and ran behind the buffet to join her friends.

"Penny, I'm constantly coming to your rescue," said a smiling Laci.

Penny's gratitude showed. "What do we do now that he has the emerald?" Penny asked Laci.

"We need your something borrowed and something blue now." Laci held out her hand.

Penny realized it was in her wristlet, which she immediately handed to Laci.

Suddenly another fireball flew over their heads and hit the table with the gifts, exploding. Laci looked back in horror as the box she'd hidden the journal in was in pieces, and the journal lay exposed out of the pillow on the ground.

"There it is!" yelled Thuban.

As he moved toward them, Ethan and Buzz set up the large slingshot. Penny and Laci loaded it with fruit and shot it at Thuban, who got some apples, oranges, and strawberries at about forty miles an hour right in the eye. It slowed him for a second but didn't stop him now that he had spotted the journal. The girls reloaded, this time with a large watermelon. He started to charge them, but they were too fast. They fired the watermelon toward his head.

Right before it hit him; he snatched it out of the air with his clawed hand and laughed at them. "Really? You're trying to defeat me with a watermelon? Thank you. You do know it's my favorite snack." He popped the watermelon into his mouth and leaned down closer to them. "Thanks, that was refreshing."

He then reached over and picked up the journal. "Come, brother, let us go home and reclaim our land!" He turned toward the kids with plans to torch them but saw that Penny and Laci faced him defiantly with their arms crossed and smiling.

"What are you smiling about?" he questioned.

"I feel an ice age coming on," Penny said.

Thuban opened his mouth, but instead of fire, a stream of ice formed. Slowly the ice covered him from head to tail; the emerald he'd wrapped in the tablecloth and the journal fell from his grasp.

Roy backed away in fear. "Brother, what have you done? Your arrogance has destroyed us!"

He was unable to escape his fate. When united, the twin brothers were joined in every way, including death. He reached his head to the sky, screaming in anger and pain, as he slowly froze, encased in his icy grave. After only a few minutes, the twins were solid ice, except for a sparkling blue light in the center of Thuban's frozen corpse.

Laci smiled at their victory. "Sapphires have always been my personal favorite."

CHAPTER TWENTY-SIX

OVER THE NEXT FEW days, Penny stayed with her grandmother to help her through the shock of it all. It was understandable that she would have a tough time adjusting to the fact that she'd unwittingly married a dragon, even though Pastor Jenkins had assured her it would be annulled. Penny made it her personal mission to rid the house of anything Roy. She filled several boxes full of his stuff that she'd either send to the Goodwill or put out in the garbage, or maybe burn in a bonfire, if Grandma would let her. Penny knew her grandmother hadn't wanted to marry a dragon, but she'd been alone for so many years, the idea of a full-time companion had made her happy, and losing that was crushing to both of them.

Most days Grandma sat in her chair looking out the front window. She hadn't been up for visitors, so Penny ran interference when anyone popped by. She knew her grandmother was grateful for that.

Penny finished sealing the last of Roy's boxes and left them in the attic until she could sneak them out of the house. She didn't want to open that wound for her grandmother by parading his few belongings in front of her.

She came down the stairs and walked into the living room to find Grandma sitting on the couch looking through a photo album.

"What's this?" she asked as she sat down next to her.

"Oh, this is just an album of old photos I came across the other day when I was clearing things out."

Penny put a comforting arm around her shoulder. Elsie turned the page and something caught Penny's eye. "Grandma, who's that?"

Grandma smiled and laughed. "That's me. Wow, that was a long time ago. I was eighteen at the time. Pretty cute, too, if I do say so myself."

"No, Grandma you were perfect!"

Grandma closed the album, stood, and asked, "Would you like some lunch?"

Penny jumped up from the couch. "No, sorry, I have to go out for a bit, but I'll be back soon." She raced past her toward the front door.

"Penny! Where are you going?"

"I need to exchange your wedding gift." Penny flew out the door with her jacket in her hand and ran all the way to Laci's house.

Outside, watering the garden, Laci saw her coming. "What's going on?" she asked.

Penny caught her breath and told her, "We have to go back."

Laci turned off the hose, opened the front door, and picked up her backpack, which sat by the door already packed. "I'm ready."

Penny laughed. "Did you have your bag already packed just in case?"

Laci looked guilty. "Maybe."

The two of them headed down the walkway, but Penny stopped and pointed at something in the garden. "Is that a jarfalla plant you were watering?"

"You can never be too prepared. Just ask Buzz," Laci said and smirked at her friend.

As they rushed back to Grandma's house, they didn't speak until they were almost there. The thought of going back to that land was both exciting and terrifying to Penny.

"Are you sure you want to travel in that? You aren't very dressed up," Laci joked to Penny.

"Thanks, but I'd like to look normal for a change," Penny responded.

"Aw, Penny, no matter what you wear, you won't fit in where we're going."

They arrived at Grandma's and entered the garage through the side door.

"Okay, we're just going there, and we'll come right back. I know you'll want to stay longer, but we can't let my grandma worry, not after what she's been through," Penny said to Laci, who reluctantly agreed. "Do your thing, girl."

Laci pulled the journal out of her backpack and thumbed through it until she found the right page. She pulled the emerald out from under her shirt, took it off her neck, and placed it on the page. A few words later, the vortex reappeared in the garage. Unlike the one that had taken them home, this one was strong and solid. They stepped into the spinning whirlpool and disappeared.

Moments later, two goats took their place. A fluffy white goat with bangs in his eyes immediately began chewing on the trashcan lid, while a black and white dappled goat gnawed on a rag.

A few hours later, the neighbor dog, Brutus, nudged his nose though the door and wandered into the garage. While the kids had been gone the weekend before last, he'd visited the garage regularly, playing with the four kittens. Elsie had taken the kittens inside once she'd discovered they were in the garage and moved them to her bathroom. While Brutus had played with the kittens, he only barked at the goats. Neither Brutus nor the goats reacted to the vortex opening up behind them. Suddenly the goats and Brutus disappeared with a flash, leaving in their place Laci, who was now wearing Hallvard's jerkin, and Penny, holding Verge's hand.

"What happened in here?" Penny asked.

"The garage is a mess," Verge said, as he looked at all the chewed-up items lying around.

Penny pulled him along out of the garage and into the house with Laci following close behind them.

"Penny, is that you? Where have you been? I've been worried sick," Grandma called from the other room. She walked out of the living room and into the kitchen to see the three of them standing there. She stood motionless when she saw the older gentleman in her kitchen.

"Elsie?" he said.

"Robert?" was all she said, and the two embraced.

"I wanted to get you a better wedding gift, Grandma," Penny said as she fought back tears.

The four of them sat down in the living room.

"I'm so confused," said Elsie.

Robert smiled and said, "Well, it's a long story, but I'll give you the condensed version for tonight." He told her about the journal and all of his amazing adventures, mainly how he had stumbled into the war between the twin dragons and the people of Botkyrka. He explained how he had worked with them to separate the brothers, one in this realm and one in their home realm. After he'd dropped Rastaban here, he'd hidden the journal and used a page from it to get back to the other land to try and destroy the other brother.

"But you can only destroy them in battle. So, if they weren't in their dragon form, you couldn't kill them," Laci said.

"I didn't know that at the time, young lady. I sure could've used your help back then." He then explained that once he'd gotten back to Botkyrka, he couldn't find the brother, but the page had been so damaged he'd been unable to get home. He'd kept an eye out to see if the brother ever discovered his journal, thus allowing him to return. He'd met various travelers while he had been stuck in the other realm but, after so many years, had given up all hope of ever returning home.

"Which brings me to a question I'm dying to ask you." Robert looked at Penny. "How did you know I was your grandfather? I never knew you existed."

Now Penny felt like the smart one. "The witches' cave."

Elsie had a terrified look.

"I saw a girl standing in front of you, and it was this girl." Penny picked up the photo album and showed him the picture of Elsie at age eighteen.

"That was taken on our first date," Robert said.

"I remember it like it was yesterday," Elsie said as she took Robert's hand and began tearing up.

Penny looked at Laci and motioned for them to go.

Leaving the two of them alone to get reacquainted, Laci and Penny sat on the porch steps.

"So was it nice seeing Hallvard again?" Penny asked.

Laci blushed. "Nice doesn't even begin to describe it," she said with a little attitude that Penny didn't normally associate with her friend's shy demeanor.

"Talk about a long-distance romance."

Laci turned an even darker shade of red. "It's not a romance. It's a special friendship. But maybe someday…"

Penny laughed.

Laci changed the subject and asked, "Where do you think Thuban put the other emerald?"

"He must have hidden it somewhere," Penny answered.

Behind them Fluffy wandered past the garage. She investigated a small brown pile. It was a pair of men's leather gloves with a lump in one of them. She batted at one glove, which caused something green to poke out of it. She sniffed the glove and ran to Penny for comfort.

As Penny petted Fluffy, she asked, "Lace, why exactly did you have Buzz shoot the emerald instead of me?"

"Trickery. I needed the shot to miss. Who better?"

The girls sat on the step, enjoying the summer evening.

Later that night, they were enjoying a hot-fudge sundae on the porch when Robert came out. "I can't thank you girls enough for what you did for me," he told them.

Penny shoveled in another helping of ice cream and fudge.

"Well, you did save our lives," Laci pointed out, then went back to her sundae.

"I think ice cream every night would be a good repayment," said Penny.

Robert sat down with them. Laci finished her sundae and grabbed her backpack. She opened it and handed the journal and the box of artifacts to Robert. "Here, this is yours," she said.

He flipped through the pages but stopped and handed it back to her. "No, the journal found you. It's yours now. Besides, I have no intention of ever leaving here again."

Laci squealed and thumbed through the book.

"Promise me you will never use it without consulting me first. I'll be able to help you navigate some of your adventures and steer you away from the pitfalls that I went through," Robert said in response to her obvious excitement.

"Look! I didn't notice this before. Here's a page that has the drawing of a feather like the one we found in Botkyrka!" Rummaging through her backpack, Laci found the book where she had place the feather for safekeeping.

Robert reached over her and took the feather out of her hands. "You girls are not ready for that yet!"

"You have got to be kidding. We just killed two dragons that you were unable to kill for over twenty years," Penny said with her usual attitude.

"Okay, fair enough, but you're not ready to travel to where this one will take you," he said as he added the feather in with the other artifacts and closed the box.

END

ABOUT THE AUTHORS

Mark Frederickson

Mark was born and raised in Southern California. He graduated UC Santa Barbara with a degree in film and has worked in the film industry for years. He has written several screenplays and had a show optioned by MTV. He lives in Los Angeles with his wife Rebecca and his daughter Sara. This is his first novel.

Melora Pineda

After Melora graduated from the UCLA School of Theater, Film and Television, she worked in the television industry for several years before becoming a volunteer at a children's library. This is her first novel. She currently lives in the Los Angeles area with her husband, daughter, bunny and fish.

ACKNOWLEDGMENTS

THANKS TO family and friends for their encouragement. Hope you enjoy reading it as much as we enjoyed writing it.

ALSO FROM BLUE TULIP PUBLISHING

BY MEGAN BAILEY
There Are No Vampires in this Book

BY J.M. CHALKER
Bound

BY ELISE FABER
Phoenix Rising
Dark Phoenix
From Ashes

BY STEPHANIE FOURNET
Butterfly Ginger

BY MARK FREDERICKSON & MELORA PINEDA
The Emerald Key

BY JENNIFER RAE GRAVELY
Drown
Rivers

BY E.L. IRWIN
Out of the Blue

BY J.F. JENKINS
The Dark Hour

BY AM JOHNSON
Still Life
Still Water

BY A.M. KURYLAK
Just a Bump

BY KRISTEN LUCIANI
Nothing Ventured

BY KELLY MARTIN
Betraying Ever After
The Beast of Ravenston

BY NADINE MILLARD
An Unlikely Duchess
Seeking Scandal
The Mysterious Miss Channing
Highway Revenge

BY MYA O'MALLEY
Wasted Time

BY LINDA OAKS
Chasing Rainbows
Finding Forever

BY C.C. RAVANERA
Dreamweavers

BY GINA SEVANI
Beautifully Damaged

BY ANGELA SCHROEDER
The Second Life of Magnolia Mae
Jade

BY K.S. SMITH & MEGAN C. SMITH
Hourglass
Hourglass Squared
Hourglass Cubed

BY MEGAN C. SMITH
Expired Regrets
Secret Regrets

BY CARRIE THOMAS
Hooked

BY RACHEL VAN DYKEN
Upon a Midnight Dream
Whispered Music
The Wolf's Pursuit
When Ash Falls
The Ugly Duckling Debutante
The Seduction of Sebastian St. James
An Unlikely Alliance
The Redemption of Lord Rawlings
The Devil Duke Takes a Bride
Savage Winter
Every Girl Does It
Divine Uprising

BY KRISTIN VAYDEN
To Refuse a Rake
Surviving Scotland
Living London
Redeeming the Deception of Grace
Knight of the Highlander
The Only Reason for the London Season
What the Duke Wants
To Tempt an Earl
The Forsaken Love of a Lord
A Tempting Ruin
A Night Like No Other

BY JOE WALKER
Blood Bonds

BY KELLIE WALLACE
Her Sweetest Downfall

BY C. MERCEDES WILSON
Hawthorne Cole
Secret Dreams

BY K.D. WOOD
Unwilling
Unloved

BOX SET — MULTIPLE AUTHORS
Forbidden
Hurt
Frost: A Rendezvous Collection

BLUE TULIP
PUBLISHING

www.bluetulippublishing.com

Made in the USA
San Bernardino, CA
10 March 2016